PERFECT HIDEAWAY

MASON CREEK, BOOK 23

BETHANY LOPEZ

Perfect Hideaway
Copyright 2022 Bethany Lopez
Published May 2022

Cover Design by Opium House Creatives
Editing by Red Road Editing / Kristina Circelli
Ebook Formatting by Bethany Lopez

This ebook is licensed for your personal enjoyment only. This ebook may not be re-sold or given away to other people. If you would like to share this ebook with another person, please purchase an additional copy for each recipient. If you're reading this ebook and did not purchase it, or it was not purchased for your use only, then please return to your favorite book retailer and purchase your own copy. Thank you for respecting the hard work of this author. All rights reserved.

All rights reserved. No part of this book may be reproduced, scanned, or distributed in any printed or electronic form without permission. Please don't participate in or encourage piracy of copyrighted materials in violation of the author's rights. Purchase only authorized editions.

This is a work of fiction. Names, characters, places, and incidents either are the product of the author's imagination or are used fictitiously, and any resemblance to actual persons, living or dead, businesses, companies, events, or locales is entirely coincidental.

This ebook is also available in print at most online retailers.

Want to learn more about my books? Sign up for my newsletter and Join my FB Group/Street Team!
http://crea.tf/bethanylopeznewsletter
https://www.facebook.com/groups/1443318612574585/

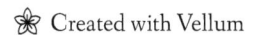

❋ Created with Vellum

Perfect Hideaway

MASON CREEK

USA TODAY BESTSELLING AUTHOR
BETHANY LOPEZ

To Kim DeVall. You are missed.

PROLOGUE

Melody

"Thanks so much for coming out tonight! I appreciate you. Drive safe."

I walked off stage, adrenaline still pumping, but exhaustion was starting to creep in.

I thanked the stagehand who handed me a water, opening it immediately and taking a long sip of the cold liquid.

I could hear footsteps behind me and figuring they were members of my band, ignored them and kept on walking toward my dressing room. It was late, about one in the morning, and I was eager to clean the makeup off my face and change into more comfortable clothing.

It had been a really great night.

My performance had felt good, everyone was on their

game, and the crowd was really into the show, which always made it better.

When I got to my dressing room, I momentarily wondered where my bodyguard was, but figured he'd turn up any second and continued inside. After closing the door, I went straight for the leggings and oversized sweatshirt I'd left out and began to pull off my cowboy boots and shimmy out of my dress.

I'd meet the band in a little bit for our traditional after-show drink, then head home to get a good ten hours of sleep.

We'd been playing five nights straight, but tomorrow we had a night off, so I fully planned to take advantage of the down time.

I was standing in my lacy bra and panty set, about to put on my clothes, when the door to my dressing room swung open with a bang.

"*Hey*," I called, automatically holding the sweatshirt in front of me as my head turned toward the door.

Both my bodyguard and manager, who were the only people I was expecting, knew to always knock and wait for my reply before opening the door. But it wasn't either of them standing in the open space staring back at me.

It was a big man with a bald head and arms the size of an elephant. He was wearing a T-shirt with my face on it and was looking at me with an expression of rapture.

"*Melody Miles*," he said reverently. "I can't believe it's really you."

"I don't know who you are, but you can't be back here," I replied with the sternest tone I could muster.

"It's me, Chris... Chris Simon. Didn't you get my letters?" he asked as if I hadn't said a word.

"*Kyle!*" I yelled, hoping my bodyguard was close by... or maybe my manager. "*Smith!*"

When no one ran in I glanced to my dressing table and saw my phone still plugged in where I'd left it charging.

"Melody," the stranger called, pulling my attention back to him. "Is it okay if I call you Melody? I feel like we know each other so well. All the letters, emails, and the present I sent. Did you get the present? I didn't get a thank you note, but that's okay. I know how busy you are... I've been to all your shows this month."

My heart was pounding, and I could feel my hands beginning to shake, but I plastered a smile on my face as I inched toward the table.

"I appreciate your support," I managed, reaching over to grab my phone in what I hoped was a nonchalant way, and unhooking it quickly.

My manager was the last person I'd texted, so I tapped out 911 and pressed send before turning my attention back to the man who was watching me with wide eyes.

"My support? I'm your biggest fan, you know that. And I know you've been wanting to see me as much as I've been wanting to see you." He took a couple steps forward and asked, "What are you doing?"

"Oh, I, ah, just had to answer a question from my manager. He gets testy if I don't reply right away," I said, taking a couple steps back and stopping when I hit the back wall.

"Can I get a hug?" he asked, coming even closer.

I was really starting to panic when I heard shouts down the hall and then both my manager and bodyguard came rushing in. Chris Simon was on the ground with his hands behind his back within seconds and my bodyguard's eyes found mine.

"Where were you?" I asked, fully shaking now.

"I got a call that there was a strange guy standing by the stage, so I went to check it out. Looks like he followed you back here without anyone seeing. I'm so sorry, Ms. Miles. I'll get him taken care of and then I'll be back to escort you home."

"I've got her," Smith assured him, before turning to me and asking, "Are you okay?"

"Can you please shut the door so I can put some clothes on?" I asked shakily.

As soon as his back was turned, I threw the sweatshirt over my head and quickly pulled on my pants. Once I was dressed, I collapsed into my chair and took a deep breath.

"What did he say to you?" Smith asked once we were alone in the secured room.

"His name is... uh... Chris Simon." I closed my eyes breathed deeply. "He's the one who's been sending letters and gifts and emails. He said he's been coming to *all* of my shows. He's been out there this whole time."

I started to hyperventilate, and Smith rushed forward to push my head between my legs. He rubbed my back while I struggled to gain control, and I felt tears prick my eyes at the realization of what could have happened.

"We can't ignore this any longer," Smith said calmly.

"I'd like you to take a break and get out of Nashville for a while. I have a buddy, Lorenzo Fratelli, he's ex-military and runs a security company. He can help you lay low and keep an eye on you until this mess with this Simon guy is solved."

I'd been giving Smith pushback about taking a break from gigs, but after my run-in with Chris Simon, I could no longer deny he was a threat. As much as I hated to take time off when things were so hot, I knew it was the smartest thing to do.

"Call him."

ONE

ENZO

"Hey, Pop, where ya at?" I called as I used my free hand to shut the front door behind me.

I'd stopped by Sal's Meats and the Mason Creek Market on my way over to grab some things for dinner, so I carried the bags toward the kitchen of the small house I'd grown up in.

The place was still decorated the way it had been when my ma died over twenty-years ago, and it was definitely starting to show its age. Wallpaper was peeling in a few places, the Formica countertops were begging for an upgrade, and the section of flooring in front of the sliding glass doors was now stained yellow.

As I was unloading the groceries, my dad came sauntering in.

"What's all this?" he asked, his eyes on the fresh vegetables I was laying out.

"I picked up some lean cuts of pork from Sal's, and I figured I'd make a salad and some brown rice to go with it."

He started to grimace, then caught my look and his face cleared.

When I'd moved back home to help him out, I'd gone with him to the doctor to learn more about his high blood pressure, high cholesterol, and borderline diabetes. Since then, I'd been helping make sure he stayed on his DASH diet, skipped the things that were bad for him, and moved around more.

At first, he'd dug his heels in and been a real pain in my ass about the whole thing, but once he started feeling better, he'd started to embrace the changes. Sure, he still fought me over bacon and caffeinated coffee, but for the most part he was being a trooper about the whole thing.

After my ma passed, his eating habits had consisted of fast food and any quick-to-make item that came in a bag, box, or can. Things had apparently only gone downhill after my brother and I left home.

But in the six months since I'd been back, he'd already lost twenty pounds and was looking and feeling much better.

"How'd the house hunting go?" he asked as he got out a cutting board and the large salad bowl.

I'd been staying at my childhood home initially, but now that I'd decided to stay and move my business to Mason Creek, I really needed my own space. It was challenging trying to find something that worked for both a business and living space, but my realtor had taken me to a couple spots earlier in the day.

"Most of them were a no go, but there are two possibilities," I told him. "I'll probably want to go back and see them again later this week. What have you been up to?"

"Walked the dog and then talked to your brother for a bit. He sounded kinda down in the dumps. Have you talked to him lately?"

I shook my head.

My brother, Gino, was only two years younger than me and we'd always been pretty close. Both of us left town after graduation to join the military. Me in the Marines, and Gino in the Army. We'd been apart over the years, but always kept in contact... first with letters, then via text and calls.

"It's been about a week," I replied. "I've been busy with work, and he's been ate up with whatever girl he's been seeing."

"I think they broke up."

I nodded. It sounded accurate. Gino was the kind of guy who fell quick and hard, without really knowing the other person or thinking of the consequences. My brother had a heart of gold but didn't always make the best decisions.

"I'll give him a call tonight," I assured my pop.

"I was trying to convince him to come visit but he said he doesn't have the leave right now."

Gino was stationed in South Carolina, which was a long haul from Mason Creek, Montana, and meant he didn't make it home much. Especially since his off time was usually spent wooing the ladies with a surprise trip.

I could tell my dad was missing him though, so I said, "I'll talk to him, see what's really going on."

"Thanks. What do you need me to do?" he asked, gesturing at the food that was now all laid out.

"You can go fire up the grill while I start chopping," I suggested.

As he was walking out back, my work phone started ringing.

"Fratelli," I said in greeting.

"Hey, Enzo... Smith. I need a favor, man. It's a work thing but needs to go into play quickly. How's your schedule right now?"

"Open," I told him, tucking my phone between my ear and shoulder as I wiped my hands and then grasped the phone. "The guys are closing up my California office now and I'm trying to settle on a new office here, so I haven't taken on anything new. What's up?"

"My client, Melody Miles, has a stalker situation which just reached red level. I need to get her out of Nashville and tuck her away somewhere safe with someone who can watch her back. I immediately thought of you and that small town you said you were moving back to."

Melody Miles was country music's current darling and since my dad was a fan, I knew she'd recently released a new album that was topping the charts.

"You thinking a few months? Do you know who the guy is? Have they caught him?" I asked, my mind going a mile a minute.

"Yeah, he showed up in her dressing room last night and is currently in custody. But she's pretty shaken up and I'd like her out of here until the dust settles and we find out what the next steps are. The pay'll be good man, well over your fee, I just need to get her out of town ASAP."

"I got you, don't even worry about it," I assured him, as I made a quick mental choice between the two properties I'd been debating over. I'd call the realtor as soon as I got off the phone to put in an offer.

In the meantime, it looked like my dad was about to have his favorite singer living under his roof until I could get into the new place.

TWO

MELODY

I rolled out of bed with a sigh.

My sleep had been fitful, as it had been the last couple nights since the incident at the venue.

Logically, I knew Chris Simon had been arrested and would not be trying to break into my house. But that didn't seem to matter to my heart, brain, or nervous system. I'd been an anxious mess ever since and I'd been doing everything I could to try and relax... Meditation, yoga, nightly aperitifs of hemp-infused non-alcoholic beverages.

Nothing had worked.

Dixie, my teacup Yorkie, started yipping from the middle of her fluffy pink pillow on my bed, so I turned back, scooped her up, and headed through the penthouse toward the patio door. Once outside, I set her down on her makeshift grass patch so she could do her business.

It was a pretty spring Nashville morning, with birds chirping and the weather just starting to gather humidity.

From where I stood, I could look out over the city and

watch it start to wake up. This was one of my favorite spots in the world, and I hated that I had to leave it, even if it was only for a short period of time.

"Come on, Dixie," I called, moving back to open the door, then waited as her little legs pranced past me inside and took her straight to her diamond-encrusted food bowl.

Once I'd started my De'Longhi La Specialista Maestro Espresso Machine, I turned back to lean against the counter and stare out my floor-to-ceiling windows while I waited for the liquid gold to fill my espresso cup.

It had taken me a while to learn how to use the machine, but my personal chef, Donna, had painstakingly explained it to me, multiple times, before I finally got it. Since I was leaving this afternoon, I'd given Donna a leave of absence. It had been hard to do, and I hoped she'd still be available when I got back, but I knew I couldn't take her with me, as much as I wanted to. She had other local clients and couldn't very well drop everything to follow me to a town in the middle-of-nowhere Montana.

I was sure I'd find a place to get my green machine smoothies and quinoa bowls.

Dixie yipped and I looked down to see her sitting pretty in front of her bowl, patiently waiting.

"Shoot. Sorry, sweetie," I said as I opened the refrigerator door and took out the food Donna made special for her.

As I was putting her food back in the fridge, my phone rang.

I saw it was my mother calling and answered it swiftly.

"Good morning," I said in greeting.

"Melody, what's this I hear about you going into some sort of witness protection?" she asked without saying so much as *hello*.

"It's not actually witness protection," I said, not wanting her to freak out. "Smith just wants me to go away for a while and let this situation get handled."

"But he said he wouldn't even tell us where you're going. I don't understand why you can't just come home."

I sighed and took my espresso off the machine.

"He's just being cautious, Mama. And I can't come home because that's the first place anyone would look."

I came from a well-known New York family, which was daily fodder for the paparazzi and gossip columns. Going back home would be no different than staying right where I was, but I could understand my mother's concern.

"I don't like it..."

"I know. But try not to worry, please. I'll be in good hands with one of Smith's friends. He has a military background and runs his own security company. And it'll only be for a few weeks." *I hope.*

"Call me all the time," she begged.

"I will. Promise."

"Okay. Have a safe trip and let me know when you get there."

"You got it," I assured her. "Love you, and love to Daddy."

"We love you, too, sweetheart."

I hung up feeling not necessarily better, but at least a little less anxious. I always felt better after talking with my mom.

I crossed through my living room, which had a large white sectional sofa, a large flat-screen TV on the wall, and my collection of guitars lining the other, intent on getting my Louis Vuitton bags out of the closet so I could start packing.

Dixie's tiny feet padded behind me, her little legs working as fast as they could to keep up. Feeling bad, as I usually did, I paused to wait for her to catch up, then picked her up and cradled her to my chest.

Once she was deposited back on her favorite pillow, I moved to get my bags and laid them out on the bed, careful not to disturb her.

I went into my large walk-in closet, which my dad said was more like another room rather than a closet and perused my things as I thought about what to pack.

Wouldn't need the fancy gowns or shoes, and I could skip all the jewelry. When I thought of Montana, I pictured jeans, cowboy boots, and other casual attire, which I had in abundance. So, I focused on picking pieces I would actually use, then threw in a couple pretty sundresses for good measure.

I was comfortable in my normal travel attire with my long auburn hair piled in a messy bun on top of my head and wearing my favorite Gucci sweatpants suit. By the time Smith arrived to pick us up, I had seven rolling bags, my makeup case, my carry-on, and Dixie's stroller and duffle waiting by the door.

Knowing me as he did, he'd brought the doorman with him along with a rolling cart.

"All set?" he asked.

I picked up Dixie, put her in the stroller, placed my hands on the handle, and replied, "As I'll ever be."

THREE

ENZO

I'd headed out early to make sure I got to the airport with plenty of time to spare.

Billings was about an hour away from Mason Creek, and sometimes the airport traffic could be heavy, especially now that we were rolling into summer.

I'd had high-profile clients like Melody Miles before, so I knew how much they hated to wait, even though they often took *their* time when the shoe was on the other foot. Still, she was one of Smith's, and I always put my client's needs ahead of my own whenever possible.

Even if they were entitled and whiny, which had been the case with a Disney Channel pop star kid I'd had to work for during some awards show. This kid had acted like I was an ant beneath his platform shoe and had gotten off on ordering me to do the most menial tasks.

Still, I'd made a couple grand off that one job and his show had gotten cancelled the next season, so I guess what goes around really does come around.

It was all part of the job. Since I loved my job, and the autonomy it gave me, I didn't complain.

Once at the airport, I waited as inconspicuously as possible for Ms. Miles to depart the plane. Because of the kind of case it was, I couldn't exactly stand there holding a Ms. Miles sign, so she'd know who I was. But I figured I'd be able to pick her out of the crowd with no problem.

All I could do was hope no one else did.

I was looking for a woman in maybe a baseball hat and glasses, wearing a T-shirt and jeans. Someone who would blend in with the rest of the travelers. What I hadn't expected was a gorgeous petite redhead who commanded attention as she strutted through the sea of people pushing a bright-pink stroller.

"*What the fuck?*" I muttered, pushing my way toward her. "So much for low profile."

Her eyes widened at my approach and when she stopped pushing the stroller, I whispered, "Come with me, Ms. Miles."

I wished I had a cap and jacket I could cover her up with, but since the weather was mild, I'd simply worn a Henley and jeans.

She blinked at me and said, "Those are my bags," and I followed her pointed finger to see an airport employee following behind her with a cart loaded with designer luggage.

Jesus.

Rather than saying anything, I simply led her out to where my F350 was waiting. Thank God my bed was empty, because the woman had no fewer than eleven bags to be loaded up.

I began tossing bags into the back of the truck, eager to get the hell out of there, while she watched me, jaw slack.

"Please, be careful," she said softly, as her suitcase landed in the back with a thud.

"It's my middle name," I retorted. Once the bags were all loaded, I moved to the stroller and said, "Smith never said anything about kids."

She blinked at me, her eyes searching my face, but didn't respond.

"Ma'am?" I prodded. "I don't have a car seat." I didn't see one with her things either, which presented a problem.

"What?" she asked, her tone conveying confusion. Then her face cleared and the most beautiful smile I'd ever seen took over. "It's not a baby, it's Dixie."

Momentarily struck by that smile, it took a moment for her words to register.

"Dixie?" I asked as she pulled what looked like a rat with hair out of the stroller. "What the hell is that?"

"A dog," she replied, kissing the rat on the nose.

"That's not a dog," I argued.

She frowned at me and held Dixie out for my inspection.

"Sure, she is. She's a teacup Yorkie and the sweetest girl in the world."

"Smith didn't say anything about any pets either."

"Oh, she's no trouble at all, I swear it."

Ms. Miles blinked those big green eyes at me once more, in a gesture that I was sure made men fall at her feet and beg to do her bidding.

Rather than argue, I simply grunted and opened her door, holding out my hand to offer her help up. She placed her hand in mine and I did my best to ignore the warm jolt that ran through me when our skin made contact.

Once she and the dog were inside, I shut the door and began to wrestle with the stroller.

"How the hell?" I grunted as I tried to get it to fold up.

"Oh, I have one of those," a man with two kids said, coming over to help me. "Just press this here and voila."

"Thanks, man," I said, shooting him a grateful smile as I put the now-folded stroller in the back. "I would've been here all day."

"No problem, they can be tricky. Enjoy the rest of your day."

"You, too," I called.

I made sure everything in the bed was secure and then moved to get in the driver's side.

"There are some drinks in the cooler," I said as I settled behind the wheel. "And unless you're hungry now, I figured we'd pick up something at Wren's once we get into town."

"That sounds good, thank you, Mr...."

"Oh *sh... shoot*, sorry," I said, scratching my head. I'd been so taken aback by her entrance at the airport that I hadn't even properly introduced myself. And she'd gotten into my truck anyway. We'd have to remedy that trusting behavior, but first, "I'm Lorenzo Fratelli, but you can call me Enzo."

She held out her hand and said, "Nice to meet you, Enzo. I'm Melody."

I gave her a sharp nod and shook her hand, before placing mine back on the steering wheel and pulling away from the no loading zone I'd been parked in.

"Let's get you to Mason Creek, *Ms. Miles*."

FOUR

MELODY

I dozed off on the drive, which was unusual. It normally took a while for me to feel safe with someone new, especially men, but there was something about Enzo that made me feel that way.

He was enormous, and kind of gruff, which should have had the opposite effect, but for whatever reason I instinctively knew I could trust him.

Dixie was snuggled on my lap, sleeping as well, when we went over some sort of bump and my eyes flashed open.

"Is this it?" I asked, charmed as we drove under a covered bridge.

"Yup, this is it. Mason Creek. A small town in every sense of the word," Enzo replied. "I'll drive through the town square so you can get the whole experience."

I sat up and looked out the window, watching the different local businesses go by. Java Jitters, Sauce it Up, One More Chapter... there was also a sub shop, beauty salon, and ice cream shop.

Enzo found a spot in front of Wren's Café and kept the engine running as he looked at me.

"I'mma grab our order and then we'll head to my pop's."

I nodded, my mind going in a million directions as I tried to take it all in.

He hopped out and I followed him with my eyes before looking over to see a bakery and a lingerie shop called Queen's Unmentionables.

There were people milling about, stopping to speak to each other periodically as they went about their business. It was like something off the Hallmark Channel, and I couldn't help but wonder what the heck I was going to do here for the next few weeks.

The café door opened and Enzo came out, pausing to hold the door for the person walking in, and I was struck by how hot he was.

Not cute, or even handsome... at least not in the traditional sense.

He was tall and built like someone who worked out. *A lot.* He had a naturally tan complexion, dark hair and dark eyes, and features that looked almost chiseled. His demeanor was intimidating, but I could see from the way he interacted with the people of his town, that he had a soft center.

And when he smiled... *Good Lord...* he had me squirming in my seat.

"All set," Enzo said as he put the bags of food in the back and returned to his seat.

We drove back through town and down one of the streets lined with houses, and seconds later, he was pulling into the driveway of a small, two-story home with blue shutters that was in desperate need of some fresh paint.

"We can go in and get settled and I'll come back out for your bags. They'll be safe here; you don't have to worry about that. The people are nosy, but they'll protect you like their own since you're staying with us."

I opened the door and eased out of the truck before Enzo had a chance to walk around and open the door for me. I could see him starting around the front, but I didn't want him to think I was some kind of diva he had to cater to. Unfortunately, when I saw how far down the pavement was, I knew I'd have a problem with Dixie in my arms.

Seconds later, Enzo was there, offering me a hand and helping me down. Usually it didn't bother me, but sometimes I really hated being short.

"Thanks," I said, glancing up at him when my feet were firmly planted on the ground, then moved around him to set Dixie down on the grass so she could relieve herself. When she finished, Enzo was waiting patiently to take us inside.

"This is your parents' house?" I asked as I followed him up the walkway.

"Yeah. My ma died when I was ten, so it was just us, and then just my dad. I just moved back a few months ago and have been staying here, but I've just closed on a new place, so we won't be staying here long."

"Oh… I'm sorry about your mom," I said lamely. I never knew how to react about the death of someone's parents, since I was lucky enough to still have my own.

Although I had written plenty of songs about it. *I'm sorry* never seemed like enough.

"Thanks, but it was a long time ago."

That may have been true, but as we walked inside, I noticed there were still family pictures everywhere. Hanging on the walls, lining tables, and adorning the mantle above the fireplace. Pictures of Enzo, his parents, and another boy I assumed was his brother.

There was a faint scent of mint and cloves and the furniture looked comfortable and well-worn.

It was the exact opposite of the penthouse I'd grown up in in New York, and exactly what I'd always envisioned a great place to grow up in would look like. No chastising when you ate food in front of the TV, or punishment when you broke your mom's good China. It felt like an actual *home*.

"Hey, Pop, we're here," Enzo called out.

We walked into the kitchen, and he put the bags of food on the counter and started to open them up.

"She's here?" I heard a man gasp and turned to see Enzo's father standing just inside the door, just in time to see him mouth my name.

His eyes were wide, and he was wringing his hands together. He was a shorter, older version of his son, but they shared the same eyes and smile. He looked adorably nervous, and I smiled kindly, immediately at ease when faced with a fan.

This I know how to deal with.

"It's so nice to meet you, Mr....?" I prompted, walking toward him.

He blinked and said, "Uh, Mario... I'm Mario."

"Hello, Mario, I'm Melody," I replied, holding out my free hand as I cradled Dixie to me with the other.

"Oh, I know. I have all your records. I love your music," he gushed, his cheeks turning rosy.

"Pops is one of the few people I know who still buys records instead of downloading or streaming online," Enzo replied from behind us. "Now stop fawning and let's eat."

"After you," Mario said, gesturing for me to walk ahead of him to the dining table.

"Thanks." I put Dixie on the ground and sat at the table while Enzo passed out plates.

"Dad's on a diet, so we've got some healthy offerings, but I also got some fried chicken, mozzarella sticks and wings, cause I wasn't sure what you liked."

"I'm a vegetarian, so I'll pass on the chicken, but I'm sure everything else will be great," I assured him, wondering why Smith hadn't said something to him beforehand.

He looked momentarily flabbergasted, then put a couple cheese sticks and some steamed vegetables on my plate.

"Thank you," I said, giving him a small smile.

But he just said, "We'll go grocery shopping in the morning," as he reached for the chicken.

FIVE

ENZO

After waking up at five and going on a six-mile run around Mason Creek, I let myself into the house intent on coffee and a shower.

Today was going to be a busy day, and although it may feel awkward for Melody to have to be by my side all day while I got things done, I didn't feel comfortable leaving her alone at my dad's.

Not that I thought she wouldn't be safe and cared for, but because without the right kind of security and a trained person in the house with her, I just didn't feel comfortable leaving her. She was a high-profile client, and I would do whatever I needed to ensure she was in good hands and no harm would come to her.

Even if that meant bringing her yappy rat along and carting them both all over town.

When I walked into the kitchen, I found Melody standing in front of the coffee machine bleary eyed and confused, the little dog prancing around her feet.

"Here, let me," I said, moving to get the coffee filter

and ground coffee out of the cupboard above the machine. She moved aside and watched as I filled the pot with water, poured it in the tank and filled the filter with grounds before pressing start.

"Not used to something so basic, princess?" I joked, my eyes flying to her face to see if she took offense. "Sorry, just slipped out."

"Huh?" she murmured, her gaze turning to me. "Oh, no... I'm used to people making assumptions about me and giving me nicknames. I barely even notice any more. And yes, I guess you could say that's accurate. I've never actually used a machine like that before, so thanks. I'm a bear without my morning cup."

Looking terribly petite in her bare feet with a shorts and T-shirt silk sleep set, she looked as far from bear-like as a person could get. Unless you were talking teddy bear. I had to admit, she did look especially cuddly right then.

Annoyed by the direction of my thoughts, I bit back a growl and said, "It'll take a few minutes to finish brewing. I'm gonna shower, then I'll make breakfast. Be ready to hit the road in an hour." Pausing at the doorway, I turned back and asked, "Do you eat eggs?'

"I do, yes. Eggs and dairy," she replied softly.

"Cool," I replied, and headed upstairs to my room.

I'd given her Gino's room to stay in for the interim, which was right across the hall from mine. I'd lit a candle in the room before we'd arrived, in hopes it would knock out any lingering smell of teenage boy that may be in there. I glanced at the door briefly as I passed but felt better with the knowledge that we would only be here for a couple more days... if I could help it.

Once I was showered and dressed in my usual uniform of jeans and a Henley, I went back down to grab my coffee and start on breakfast.

I noticed my dad was sitting out on the back porch with Melody, so I grabbed the rolled oats out of the pantry and put them on the counter next to the eggs, veggies and wheat toast. He would not be getting eggs but could have everything else on his diet.

Once the omelets, oatmeal and toast were done, I took a plate for each of them outside and placed them in front of them.

"Oh, you don't have to wait on me," Melody protested. "I can get my own food, and even help with the cooking if you'd like."

"It's no problem, I was making breakfast anyway," I assured her. "But I may take you up on the cooking help. Now that we have to make everything from scratch it feels like a full-time job."

"Why does she get eggs?" my dad grumbled when he compared their plates.

I grinned at his insolence. He was usually a good sport about it, but sometimes this diet made him grumpy.

"Sorry, Pops. She can have eggs because she doesn't have high cholesterol."

He scowled in response, but I just laughed and turned to go back in and get my own plate.

I joined them, and after a while the silence was becoming awkward, until Melody asked, "Is your brother out of town... the one whose room I slept in?"

"Uh, no, not exactly. I mean, technically, yes, but Gino left home over ten years ago to join the Army. Dad never changes anything, so our rooms have been the same for the last decade and a half at least."

"Were you also in the Army?" she asked, spearing a strawberry with her fork.

"Marines," I replied. "I joined right after high school and served eight years. Then me and some of my buddies decided to open our own security company, and the rest is history."

"You said you recently moved back…"

"He came back to help me out around here. Or maybe it was just cause he liked the idea of bossing me around as some kind of payback," my dad replied, pushing his oatmeal around with his spoon without actually eating any.

"Come on, Pop," I chided, then glanced at Melody, who was smiling at my father. "We started the business in California, got a lot of Hollywood clients, which built us up pretty quickly. Now that we're established, we can run things from anywhere, so when the doctor told me what was going on with my pops, I decided our main base would be here in Mason Creek. We'll still have a small office in LA, which one of my guys, Murray, will run, but everyone else is coming out here. There's often quite a bit of travel, but this will be home when we aren't on the road."

"And once he gets his own place maybe I'll get a little peace around here."

I shot my dad a look but didn't reply. There was no use arguing with him when he was in one of his moods. I could understand being frustrated when you couldn't do the things you were used to doing. And I didn't want to bring up the fact that once I wasn't living here, I'd be hiring a nurse to come in and check on him daily. It would just fire him up even more.

SIX

MELODY

We finished eating and Mario insisted on cleaning up so we could get going, so I hurried upstairs to get myself ready for the day.

Knowing we were simply running errands and it wasn't like my usual day filled with interviews, meetings, and constant public scrutiny, I put on minimal makeup, pulled my hair back into a ponytail, and threw on a simple maxi dress.

It felt kind of nice knowing paparazzi wouldn't be waiting outside to follow me everywhere, hiding in bushes, or snapping pictures of me with my mouth full of food.

When I was back downstairs, about to grab Dixie's bag and stroller, Enzo looked from me to the dog and said, "Maybe she could hang out with Pops for a while. I don't think the grocery store will feel too keen on having her wandering the aisles."

"Oh," I said, glancing down at my sweet baby in my arms. "You stay here with Mario, okay?"

She tilted her head as she looked at me as if trying to decipher what I was saying, and my heart swelled.

"Are you sure he won't mind?"

"Pop, can you watch the dog?" Enzo shouted through the house.

"Yeah!" Mario yelled back. "No problem. I'll take her for a walk."

I followed the sound of his voice to the living room and laid Dixie down in his lap.

"Her leash and treats are in her little pink backpack by the door."

"She'll be fine," he promised with a small smile, and the way he held her close let me know she would be.

Our first stop was the Mason Creek Market.

"I need to try and find some food for Dixie," I told Enzo as he grabbed a cart.

"I'm sure whatever kibble she usually eats is in stock here. We're not that remote."

"Oh, she doesn't eat regular dog food. My chef usually cooks her meals along with mine, so I need to find something comparable, so she doesn't get an upset tummy."

Enzo stared at me for a moment, without saying a word, and I realized I'd seen him do this a few times already. With me, and with his dad, and I figured it meant he was taking a beat so he wouldn't say anything he'd regret.

I thought it was a sweet and funny habit, but also that it meant he knew himself, and how to handle communication, very well. Most people I knew didn't have such restraint.

I was sure he thought Dixie and I were a bit ridiculous, but he remained professional and took everything in stride. I liked that about him. I also liked the way he filled out his jeans.

Bad, Melody! I mentally chastised myself and sent him a sunny smile.

He simply grunted and started pushing the cart down the aisles.

"Grab whatever you need for your meals, and for the dog," he told me as we moved quickly through the store.

At the pace he was going, I'd never find a thing, so I suggested we split up and meet back at the front of the store. At first, he protested. "I don't like the idea of leaving you alone," he'd said. But I assured him I'd be fine in the small store and promised to yell for him if something made me feel uncomfortable.

After a few minutes of a silent stare-down, he'd relented.

Once alone, I loaded up on fruits and fresh veggies, as well as some other staples in my daily routine. In the dog aisle, I found a brand called *FreshPet* in a small refrigerator and hoped it would be similar to what Dixie was used to.

"Ms. Miles?" a voice said tentatively from behind me.

I turned to see a tall, lovely blonde woman who was smiling at me prettily and cradling her very pregnant belly.

"Yes?" I asked cautiously. Just because no one was supposed to know I was here didn't mean the people who lived here wouldn't recognize me, I reminded myself when my heartbeat sped up.

"Hi, I'm Faith. Faith Collins. My husband and I ran into Enzo, and he said you were back here looking for something for your pet rat."

I chuckled and shook my head. "She's actually a dog. A teacup Yorkie. I don't know why he insists on calling her a rat. He seems to think unless it weighs a hundred pounds, it doesn't qualify as a dog."

"Oh, how sweet. I'd love to meet her, and I know my daughter, Hope, would, too. She's seven and just loves animals."

"Dixie loves kids," I replied.

"Anyway, I just wanted to come over, introduce myself, and welcome you to Mason Creek. Also, since you're new here, I thought you might like to join me and some of my friends for brunch on Sunday. Just a small get-together, but you could have a mimosa and meet some people."

"Oh, I don't drink alcohol, and I'm not sure if I should. I'd need to talk with Enzo," I said lamely, unsure of what he'd told her and her husband about me and what I was doing here. *Was he just going to tell everyone he was my security, or was there some sort of covert cover story?* I had no idea and should probably find out.

"Well, here... I'll give you my card. I own Serenity Salon in the square, so if you ever need a touch-up, give me a call. And do so if you change your mind about brunch as well."

"I will. Thank you. And it was lovely meeting you," I said, stuffing the business card into my purse.

Fifteen minutes later I got to the registers to find

Enzo standing there next to his basket, looking down at his phone.

Seeing him like that, unaware of being watched and not standing stiffly at high alert as he seemed to do, I realized how devastatingly handsome he was. I noticed a few other women checking him out as they went past and got in line at checkout, but he was oblivious to the stares.

As I stepped closer, his head swung up and his eyes met mine, and I found myself momentarily breathless at the intensity of those dark eyes.

"You find everything you need?" he asked, his deep voice giving me chills.

"Mmm-hmm," was all I could manage as I nodded like an idiot.

I was not used to feeling so off center around anyone, let alone a man.

"Great, then let's check out and beat feet."

SEVEN

ENZO

I turned my truck onto the long gravel road which eventually turned into the driveway that led down to the converted warehouse I'd put a bid on. It was on five acres of land with trees lining the borders of the property, which would give me the privacy I desired.

"Now you have to use your imagination a bit," I said as we got out of the truck, feeling excited as all of my ideas swam around my head. "Once we close, I'll have a large team here for about a week, working night and day to see my vision come together so that we can move in as soon as possible. I'll probably have them start with the residential space, so we can be here during construction. The security system I'm putting in this place will make it like a fortress."

I saw her lips turn up, probably over my so far uncharacteristic enthusiasm, but she simply nodded and let me lead her up the path to the front of the building.

"Okay, so through here will be offices, a large workout space, and a kind of command center. Then through these doors, I'll have an assortment of dorm-like rooms for the guys who aren't living here... the guys who do will probably buy or rent their own places... but the ones who are only in town for a short period will be able to stay here on site. Now, upstairs," I said as I led her up. "This will be my personal apartment."

I opened the sliding door, which went up like a garage door, and stepped aside to let her in.

"Wow, this is huge," she said appreciatively as she walked past.

"Down here will be the common areas. Kitchen, breakfast nook, and living room, and I'll have a nicer stairwell put in leading up to the loft where my bedroom will be. I'm thinking a bathroom on each level."

I took her up to the loft area, telling her to, "Watch your step," as we went up the old metal staircase. Then we moved to the far side of the room and out the window to climb up the paragon stairs which went up to the roof.

"Now this is my favorite part," I told her when we reached the top.

The previous owners had sectioned off a space for a rooftop terrace, which I would absolutely be updating and utilizing myself.

"I'll have some greenery put in and maybe a water feature. But there will be an outdoor bar with comfortable patio furniture and some sort of covering... maybe bamboo... I don't know yet, I'm still planning it all out."

"This is amazing," Melody said, crossing to stand near the edge of the roof and look out over the property. "Oh, look, there's a pond."

"Yeah, I was thinking I'd put out some benches or a

picnic table over there for when the guys want to enjoy the outdoors."

I turned to look down at her, catching her profile as she serenely took in the area.

"So, what do you think?" I asked, even though I wasn't sure why her opinion mattered so much. It wasn't like she was going to be here long term.

"It's a really special place," she said, shading her eyes with her hand as she looked up at me. "You have great ideas and the way you describe it; I can picture it perfectly. I'd love to help out in any way I can while I'm here."

"Thanks, I just may take you up on that."

We headed back downstairs, making it into the commercial space as my realtor was walking inside.

"I hope you don't mind, we let ourselves in," I said, crossing to shake his hand.

"It's no problem," he replied easily, giving Melody a smile and nod. "It looks like everything is going to go off without a hitch and you'll be coming to the office to sign a ton of paperwork by the end of the week."

"Perfect," I said, then gestured to Melody and said, "This is my client, Melody."

"Of course, I know who you are. My wife and I are big fans," he said, looking a little embarrassed.

"Thank you so much." She gave him a bright smile and allowed him to take a selfie with her, while I said, "Her time here in Mason Creek is on the down low, so please do not share that with anyone outside of town or post it anywhere. At least until she's back safely in Nashville."

"Of course, Enzo. Your instructions have been passed through the rumor mill. Heck, Tate even included them in the latest issue of the Mason Creek Scoop. The whole town knows of Ms. Miles' situation and will guard her privacy with our lives."

"Oh, I'm sure that's not necessary," Melody said quickly, looking alarmed.

I grinned at her and said, "He just means they'll keep the fact that you're living here a secret. There's no reason to believe any harm will come to anyone. But I'd rather err on the side of caution. Call it one of the hazards of the job."

"We're all thrilled to have you here."

"Speaking of which," I said, turning to look down at Melody. "I ran into my buddy Mitch at the grocery. I think his wife, Faith, found you?" She nodded in response. "Well, he suggested we meet up at Pony Up tonight."

"What's that?" she asked.

"Local stomping grounds. It's the only bar in town, so you'll meet most everyone there at one point or another. There's even live music tonight, which I thought may interest you."

"That sounds wonderful. I can't remember the last time I was at a bar where I wasn't the one performing."

"I'll text him and let him know we're in then."

"Do you think your dad will mind watching Dixie again?" she asked, chewing her bottom lip in such a way that I momentarily lost my train of thought.

"Well, uh," my realtor said, clearing his throat

awkwardly. "I guess I'd better motor... I've got another client to meet."

"Yeah, sorry, man, we'll be heading out too," I told him, and we all walked outside.

We waived him off and started to get in the truck, when I remembered I hadn't answered Melody's question.

I appreciated that rather than asking again she'd waited for me gather myself. But I hoped she hadn't seen me staring at her lips.

"As far as my dad goes, I'm sure he won't mind. He probably enjoys having her around to keep him occupied. Maybe I should get him a dog... or a cat," I mused as I turned the engine.

"Or a rat," Melody teased.

EIGHT

MELODY

I decided on country bar chic for my first night out in Mason Creek.

Floral above-the-knee dress with denim jacket and cowboy boots. I had my long auburn hair in low pigtails which cascaded down my chest and makeup that was feminine but not too heavy.

It felt good getting dolled up, since I'd been mostly rocking yoga pants and hoodies since arriving.

When I got downstairs, I found Enzo in the living room with his dad. He was bent slightly at the waist scratching Dixie behind the ears, and when he heard me enter, he straightened quickly, snatching his hand back as if he'd been caught doing something wrong.

He'd swapped out his Henley for a black button-up shirt and he'd styled his hair a little differently.

"You look nice," I told him, crossing to pick Dixie up and give her a snuggle.

"So do you," Enzo replied gruffly.

"You kids have fun," Mario said with a grin as I handed my baby back to him.

"Will do," Enzo said.

"Thanks. And thanks for taking care of Dixie."

"It's no problem," Mario assured me.

We left and took the short drive to the bar, which was on the far corner of town. The parking lot behind Pony Up was packed and I felt a jolt of nerves in my stomach.

"Looks busy," I noted.

"Yeah, a lot of people show up over the weekend to unwind and hang out. Plus, Tucker's playing tonight, and he usually draws a crowd."

I knew a lot of Tuckers, so I didn't think anything of it, until we walked inside, and my eyes adjusted to the dark space.

"Oh, I know him!" I exclaimed when I first heard, and then saw him up on stage. "Tucker Simms... what is he doing here?"

"He lives here," Enzo replied, his eyes curious. "How do you know him?"

"He wrote one of the songs on my last album. We met in Nashville. I guess I just assumed he lived there."

"He's not from here, and he moved here while I was gone, but he's a stand-up guy. Great musician." Enzo pointed toward the bar. "Let's go get a drink. You can go say hi when he takes a break."

I nodded and kept my eyes on the stage as we moved through the crush of bodies.

When we got to the bar, Enzo indicated I should go first, so when the bartender leaned in to ask what I'd like,

I stepped up on the footrest so that I could be close enough for him to hear me.

"Do you have *Aplós* or *The Pathfinder*?" I asked, speaking loudly to be heard over the music. I knew it was a longshot, but I figured it didn't hurt to ask.

She shook her head and asked, "What kind of alcohol is that honey? Never heard of em."

"They're actually non-alcoholic, hemp-based spirits," I replied in a rush, before quickly adding, "I don't drink alcohol. Can I have a club soda with lime?"

"You got it," she said, then looked to my right and asked, "Enzo?"

"A double Makers, please."

When she went to make our drinks, Enzo leaned over and asked, "Are you hungry? I don't think they have any of that Impossible stuff, but they have plain nachos with cheese."

"I'm okay, thanks," I replied, pleased that he seemed to take my dietary restrictions in stride.

It was funny how many people acted like I was high maintenance simply because I didn't eat meat or drink alcohol. I never judged anyone for doing so or made a big deal over what they were ordering, but for some reason, I wasn't always afforded the same courtesy.

In Nashville, I had my favorite places to go where they served what I was looking for, but it was always difficult when I was traveling, or when I was invited to an event.

It was like my life choices made others uncomfortable with their own.

Once we had our drinks, we made our way closer to

the stage and were lucky enough to have a two-top open up.

A few people came over to say hello and Enzo introduced me. Everyone was really nice and although I could see the excitement over meeting a "celebrity" on some of their faces, no one got too close or went fangirl over me.

I was able to meet Mitch, Faith's husband, who said Faith's pregnancy was making her feel uncomfortable, so she'd decided to stay home. He was eager to get back to her but wanted to stop and reiterate her invitation to brunch.

"She said she'd kill me if I didn't tell you, and right now, I believe her," Mitch had said with a chuckle.

"I'll give her a call," I promised.

The music faded out and Tucker said he was taking a break, so I told Enzo I'd be back and went to say hi.

"Tucker," I called when he was about to walk off stage.

His head swung around, and it took him a moment to register that it was me, here, outside of Nashville, and then his face cleared, and he grinned.

"*Melody Miles*, what the heck are you doing here?" he asked, moving swiftly to pull me in for a quick hug.

He was tall, *okay, everyone's taller than me*, and handsome, with a neatly trimmed beard and his signature ball cap atop his head.

"I'm not sure if you heard," I began quietly, not wanting to make an announcement to the room even though according to Enzo, most of the people of Mason Creek already knew. "I had an... episode... with a stalker after one of my shows. My manager thought it would be good for me to get out of town and hide away somewhere safe while the whole situation gets dealt with. I'm staying with Enzo," I said, pointing over to where Enzo was sitting and talking to some pretty blonde, which gave me a moment's pause before I remembered what I was saying and turned my attention back to Tucker. "He's my current head of security."

"No, I hadn't heard, that's terrible," Tucker said, his face filled with concern. "I haven't known him long, but Enzo's a good man and I've only heard good things about his security business. I'm glad you're okay, and I hope you're enjoying Mason Creek so far, despite the reason you came."

"I am. It's a nice change of pace."

"You'll have to come over for dinner," he said with an easy smile. "Meet Justine and Matthew. I know they'd both love it."

"That sounds great," I said, meaning it. "Maybe you can show me what you've been working on."

"Anytime. And if you're up to it, I'd love to invite you onstage for a song tonight."

"Yeah, sure. It's been a couple weeks since all this happened, and it would be great to feel some normalcy."

"Perfect. The crowd will love it. How about *Don't you wanna stay*?" he asked.

"It's one of my favorites."

NINE

ENZO

I laid in bed the remembering the way Melody had looked up on that stage the other night.

It was like watching a metamorphosis. She completely transformed from the quiet woman who seemed slightly nervous and unsure of her place in this town, to a woman who knew she was exactly where she belonged, doing what she'd been born to do.

Tucker'd sat on his stool with his guitar, while she'd stood behind the mic stand, and they'd belted out the popular Kelly Clarkson and Jason Aldean tune.

Her stage presence was enthralling, and as she sang with that small knowing smile on her lips, I'd been utterly captivated. She was the sexiest person I'd ever seen and from the moment she opened her mouth until the last note was sung, I'd simply sat there transfixed.

I'd been unable to fall asleep that night and had tossed and turned until I'd finally wrapped my hand around my cock and relieved the ache that had been plaguing me for the last week.

I wasn't big on serious relationships, but I'd had regular sexual partners back in California. Since I'd been back home, that had not been the case. Not only because I was first focused on my dad, and then on moving my business halfway around the world, but because I knew everyone in Mason Creek.

The relationships from my youth were not anything I wished to revisit, and I simply didn't feel right having a casual fling with someone I would literally have to run into all the time. I was running on a dry spell, so my attraction to Melody was only normal.

She was a gorgeous, talented woman, and because it had been so long, I couldn't help but want her.

It didn't have anything to do with how she was as a person... *sweet, funny, and surprisingly kind and self-aware...* It was chemistry, plain and simple. And since she was a client, I would never act on it.

Unfortunately, my body hadn't received the memo.

I groaned, cursed under my breath, and got out of bed, intent on a nice hot shower, but when I opened the door, the first thing I saw was Melody coming out of the bathroom, steam billowing behind her, clad only in a towel.

"*Fuck,*" I muttered, and slammed my door shut.

I took a few deep breaths and ordered myself to ignore the glimpses of rosy skin I'd seen, then when I heard her bedroom door shut, I reopened mine and crossed to the bathroom.

It smelled of lavender and honey and my dick was so hard it was painful, but luckily or not, she'd used all the hot water, so the cold spray helped dampen my desire.

Ten minutes later I was practically frozen and wide awake.

I went back into my room to get dressed and saw I had a missed call from Tank, my number two. Since he was heading up the move and they were supposed to be on the road by the beginning of the week, I quickly picked up the phone and called him back.

"Hey, man," he said when he answered.

"Hey. Sorry I missed you, I was in the shower. What's up?" I asked, tucking my phone between my ear and my shoulder as I struggled to put my boxer briefs on.

"Not much, I just wanted to give you an update," Tank said, and I could hear the sound of a woman in the background.

I looked at the clock and wondered why he was already up and calling, especially if he had someone in his bed.

Tank was a notorious night owl, the opposite of me, which was why he was my number two. I could always count on him to take charge of things when I wasn't around. But that meant he never usually got going until after noon.

"Dude, it's like nine there, what are you doing up?" I asked.

He lowered his voice and said, "I can't get this babe to leave. She woke up and started talking about brunch... freaked me out. So, I told her my boss had stuff for me to do."

He'd been in a war, but brunch freaked him out...

I chuckled and replied, "Well, it's partially true. You *are* moving an entire business. Just tell her you have to get some last-minute stuff done and you're on a deadline."

"I tried that... she offered to help," he whispered, then said loudly, "Yes, sir. Right away. I know how important this is."

Him calling me *sir* made me snort, then I said, "You're not cut out for the one-night stand life. You're always too worried about hurting their feelings. Just tell her you gotta go and let me know once everything's done and you're on your way."

"Sorry, sweetheart," he told the mystery woman. "I'm afraid brunch is out of the question. I've gotta go meet up with a couple of the guys and get this done."

Tank had been in a long-term relationship but during our last deployment his wife had left him for their landscaper, and he hadn't been the same since. He'd never been the love 'em and leave 'em type, and I could tell he still wasn't comfortable in the role.

"That's why I called, thanks again, sir. I won't let you down," Tank said, even though I hadn't said anything, then added, "You got it, boss."

"See, you didn't even need me," I told him.

"Thanks, sir, I'll call you later."

I rolled my eyes to the heavens and disconnected the call, then finished getting dressed.

I had my own work to get done this morning. First, I'd be signing all the closing paperwork and then I was meeting with the contractors so they could get started. It was going to be a rush job, which meant a good deal of money, but it was important to me to get everything done quickly so we'd be ready when the guys got here.

Melody was meeting Faith and some of her friends for brunch, so we'd get a little reprieve from each other, which with how much she kept intruding on my thoughts, seemed like a good thing.

TEN

MELODY

"Oh my gosh, you're even sexier in person! How is that possible?" A beautiful blue-eyed blonde about my age exclaimed when I tried to sneak quietly into the brunch.

"Right," Faith said, pushing herself up and out of her chair to come toward me. "Like a gorgeous, auburn-haired pixie."

I felt my cheeks redden as everyone in the salon turned to look at me.

When I'd gotten back with Faith about the brunch, she told me it was a quarterly thing they held in her salon. They ordered in food, and everyone came to enjoy mimosas and bloody Marys and catch up without the prying eyes of Mason Creek on them.

"Oh, you didn't have to get up," I told Faith as she brought me in for a quick hug and air kiss.

"No worries, it's good for my legs to keep moving," she said, waving off my protest. "I'm so glad you decided to come. Here, let me introduce you."

Faith urged me closer to the long table which I guessed was actually a couple of folding tables pushed together so that everyone could sit together. The attendees were all women, and one young girl, and they were all looking at me with welcoming smiles.

"Ladies, I'm sure she needs no introduction, but just in case... this is Melody, and she's in town staying with the Fratellis while she lays low. You all heard about what happened in Nashville and know Enzo has requested we keep her time in town discreet, so please no pictures on social media."

Everyone murmured their agreement and gave shouts of, "*Hello*", "*hey*", and "*welcome.*"

I was seated next to Faith and the blonde, who was introduced as Olivia, the owner of Queen's Unmentionables and Faith's best friend.

"And that little firecracker on the other side of Olivia is Hope, my daughter," Faith said.

"Hi, Hope," I said, lifting my hand in a wave.

Rather than reply, Hope scooted out of her chair and came running around the table to stand next to me. She was adorable with her hair in uneven pigtails and mismatched shoes on her feet.

"My mommy says you have a doggie. I have a cat. Her name is Prince Alice, and she doesn't like dogs."

"Yes, I do, want to see a picture?" I asked.

When she nodded enthusiastically, I pulled out my phone and showed her the lock screen, which was a photo of Dixie.

"*Ohhh, she's so cute*," Hope cried.

"She is, and she's so tiny that I bet even Prince Alice

would like her, because she is probably bigger than Dixie."

I showed her a few more pictures and then Faith told her to go sit back in her seat and eat some food.

"Would you like a mimosa or a Bloody Mary?" the woman next to me asked.

"Just some orange juice or coffee, if you have some," I replied.

"We have both," she replied sunnily, passing the two carafes to me. "I'm Cheryl, I'm one of the stylists who work here with Faith."

"It's nice to meet you, Cheryl."

"You, too, and there's something I've been dying to ask you," she said, her eyes widening.

Thinking she was going to ask me something about my singing career, one of the guys I'd toured with, or Nashville in general, I gave her a small smile and nodded.

"Sure, go ahead."

"What is it like living with Enzo?" she gushed.

There were a few sounds of agreement from around the table and even a couple longing sighs.

I looked around at the women who had probably known Enzo all their lives, or at the very least, much longer than I had, and wasn't sure what to say. I didn't know if anyone in this room had a history with him, or even what his reputation was in the community.

So, I hesitated...

"Don't worry, what you say here, stays here," one brunette promised.

"Yeah, we won't tell..."

"You can be honest with us."

Faith laughed and said, "Come on, guys, don't put her on the spot." Then she looked at me and said, "Don't worry, no one at this table has ever dated him, or even came close, right ladies?"

Everyone agreed, and although I felt a bit awkward, I admitted, "He's been really great, taking me in the way he has, even though I realize he's getting paid to do so. Still, he's made me feel comfortable, and safe. Although, he can be a bit... *frustrating*."

"Like, in a sexy way?" someone asked, and everyone laughed.

I wasn't sure how to respond, so I said, "Of course, he is attractive. But he's also kind of hard to read and he doesn't say a whole lot. We're, like, complete opposites."

"Are there any sparks between the two of you? I mean, they do say... opposites attract," Olivia asked, resting her chin on her hand and leaning across the table. "Cause I saw the way he was looking at you at the Pony Up, and...*damn*. I got turned on just from watching."

I blinked and met her eyes.

"He was watching me?" Then I shook my head and said, "He's in charge of my security."

"Yeah. And the way his eyes were, well, let's just say there wasn't anything *professional* about it. It was like he was trying to remove your clothes, layer by layer, with just a look. It was hella hot."

"Hmm," I murmured, thinking back to that night. I couldn't deny we had chemistry between us, and the more time I spent around him, the more *fantasies* I seemed to conjure up whenever I had a moment to myself.

Of course, I couldn't say that to these women, who I barely knew, before I figured out what, or if, I wanted to do about it.

"I am a little in love with his dad," I said with a smile, hoping they'd let the conversation go.

"Mario Fratelli is a total sweetheart," Faith agreed.

"He is," Olivia said, her tone sad. "I felt so bad for him after his wife died. He's never seemed to recover from it."

"I, for one, would be happy to help him out," Cheryl said with a lascivious wink. "Those Fratelli men are prime specimens... *all* of them!"

"*Cheryl*," one of the women chided. "You're so bad."

Everyone laughed and the conversation moved on, and I was very glad to be out of the spotlight for once.

ELEVEN

ENZO

I was on the back patio, drinking my coffee as I mentally prepared for the day ahead.

It was officially moving day. Construction was complete, the guys would be arriving from California with the truck, and I had a small U-Haul trailer for the little bit of stuff I needed to take with me from my dad's.

The last couple weeks had gone by in a flash of shopping, which I hated, and lots of late nights.

Melody had been awesome, helping me with the little details I couldn't care less about, but she assured me were important. When she hadn't been helping me, she'd been locked up in Gino's old room writing songs and playing her acoustic guitar.

When my phone rang and I saw it was my brother, I muttered, *"Finally,"* and quickly answered.

"Gino, what the hell, man, I've been leaving you messages for weeks," I said instead of a greeting

"I know, sorry. I've just been in a bit of a funk and doing my best to get out of it," came his reply.

"Everything okay?" I asked, worried. My brother was usually an easygoing guy. Not much phased him or put him in a *funk*. "Pops said something about a girl. Was it that serious?"

Gino sighed and said, "Yeah. At least... I thought it was. But look, that's over now and I'm moving on. I was calling to tell you I may be coming home in a few weeks."

I grinned, excited about the prospect of seeing him and at the knowledge our dad would be elated.

"That's great, brother. It'll be good for us all to be together. But Dad said you didn't have the leave..."

"I don't, but since I decided not to reenlist, it doesn't really matter," he said softly, his tone conveying his worry over sharing this news.

"Last I heard you were in it for the long haul."

"Yeah, well, things change. And I know this may not be what you and Pops want, but it's what I think is best for me."

"So, you're coming home for good?" I asked, my head brimming with possibilities as it caught up with his words. "That'll be great. I've been feeling bad about leaving Pops alone, even though he'll have a nurse and I'll be five minutes away. If you stay here and help him out that would really be a load off. Plus, you know I'm moving the business out here. The guys will be getting here today, and there's always a job waiting for you if you want it."

Gino was silent for a few beats, then said, "Thanks, Enzo, it really means a lot."

"Hey, we're family," I said simply because, really, that said it all.

"Yeah," my brother murmured, then his voice picked up and he sounded more like himself when he added, "Pops said Melody Miles is staying at the house. Is she as pretty in person as she is on TV?"

I chuckled and leaned back in my chair as I looked into the house where she was pouring herself a cup of coffee.

She looked rumpled and befuddled, like she did every morning right after she woke up and before her first cup. It's funny how quickly I'd become used to these little pieces of her and was starting to find comfort in them.

"Better," I replied with a grin.

"Man... I can't wait to meet her," Gino said. "I think we're about the same age."

"Don't even go there," I said, my tone a little too harsh as I sat up straight in my seat. "She's off limits."

Gino's laugh filled my ear.

"So that's how it is..."

"No," I replied with a scowl. "She's a client. And one of the first rules you'll learn when you come work for me, is that clients are off limits."

"Mm-hm, sure," he joked, and I swear it was as if he were sitting right in front of me and I could see him winking.

I growled just as the sliding glass door opened and Melody came out, pausing to let Dixie hop out the door after her, before shutting it and taking a seat.

I moved the phone from my ear and said, "Good morning."

"Morning," she replied, then gave a dainty little yawn.

Dixie trotted to the grass, did her business, and then started to try and climb the stairs again, but her legs were so short she couldn't quite make it.

Since Melody was currently fueling herself with coffee, I got up to help the little rat up the stairs.

"Oh, is that her? Maybe I should Facetime so we can meet face to face," Gino said smoothly.

"This conversation is over," I told him gruffly. "Let me know when your travel plans are set. Do you want to tell Pops, or do you want me to?"

"I'll call him later, but you can tell him," Gino said, then added, "Can't wait to see you, bro. And to be home."

"Yeah, me too. Talk soon," I replied, then disconnected the call and dropped Dixie in Melody's lap before taking my seat. "That was my brother, Gino. Looks like he'll be coming to town soon."

Melody perked up a little at that.

"Oh really, wow, I kinda feel like I know him, being in his room and all. I can't wait to actually meet him."

"He's a good guy, and my dad's gonna be thrilled."

"That's good. I feel bad leaving your dad here alone," she said, mirroring my earlier thoughts. "I think he's really going to miss Dixie. They've gotten pretty close."

I nodded and said, "I've been thinking I should get him a pet. Maybe a cat, since they're a bit easier to take care of... more self-sufficient."

"Oh, I bet he'd love that. A sweet little kitten." Her face got soft just thinking about it.

I chuckled and said, "You can help me pick one out."

"*Yay!*" she exclaimed, clapping her hands together,

which startled Dixie into standing up and barking. To which, Melody murmured, "Sorry, baby."

"It'll have to be another day, though, since today's going to be a busy one. Have you decided if you want to hang out here or at the compound?"

I'd started calling the space *the compound*, since it was more than a house or office, and the name seemed to fit.

"I'd like to come with you and help out with the unpacking and stuff, if that's okay. If you think I'll be in the way I can hang back," she said, her eyes hopeful.

"You won't be in the way," I assured her. "But if you want to come this train will be leaving in ten."

Melody hopped up, tucked Dixie under one arm, and said, "I'll be ready."

I followed her back into the house, rinsed out our cups and put them in the dishwasher, then put together a breakfast of fruit, oatmeal, and herbal tea for my dad, and went to tell him the good news.

TWELVE

MELODY

When we got to Enzo's new place it was already teeming with people.

We walked into the bustle of activity to find the contractors finishing up some last-minute details Enzo had found that needed to be fixed, two moving trucks containing Enzo's business stuff and his men, and the interior designer, Ashley, who I'd been working with.

Enzo had told me what his ideas were and said I could expand on that, as long as I didn't go too crazy and stayed within budget.

It had been a great way to take my mind off everything I was missing out on back in Nashville. I'd been splitting my time between working with Ashley and writing new music. I'd even been able to meet with Tucker a few times to run through the new stuff and we were working on something together.

Surprisingly, once I sat down and thought about it, I found the break from the grind was doing me good and being able to have these creative outlets was only helping with the flow of song writing.

Also, it didn't hurt to have inspiration such as Enzo. I was finding him to be a pretty perfect muse, although I hadn't said any such thing to him.

"Hey man, good to see you."

I watched Enzo embrace one of the biggest men I'd ever seen in one of those manly half-hug, half back slap things.

"It's been too long, brother," the large gentleman agreed with a happy grin.

"Tank, this is Melody Miles," Enzo said when I slowly shuffled over, "Melody, this is the greatest guy I know."

"Nice to meet you, ma'am," he said, gently enveloping my small hand in his large one. "You're under the protection of the best in the business."

"I pay him to say that," Enzo joked, looking lighter than I'd seen him. "Literally."

I laughed and said, "It's nice to meet you, Tank. Is that a nickname, or…"

"Yes, ma'am. Name's actually Stanley, but my fellow Marine's said I looked more like a tank than a Stanley, and the nickname stuck."

"It does fit you well," I agreed, thinking I'd never seen anyone look *less* like a Stanley. "Well, I'll let you two catch up and go check in with Ashley."

I left them alone and found Ashley back in the residential part of the building putting out some last-minute touches.

"Good morning."

She looked up from the flower arrangement she was finishing, a tall, beautiful woman with tan skin, brilliant white teeth, and a keen fashion sense.

"Good morning, Ms. Miles."

I'd asked her a million times to call me Melody, but she never did.

"Everything looks wonderful," I gushed as I looked around the space. It was minimalist, with clean lines done in gray and cream, and looked just masculine enough to appease Enzo, but still pretty and functional.

"Thank you," Ashley said, coming toward me with her hands clasped in front of her. "I have a little surprise for you. Enzo had me working on it in secret but said I could do the big reveal this morning."

"A surprise?" I asked, honestly stunned and unsure what she could mean.

"Yes, follow me."

We walked through the living room and kitchen to a back area underneath the loft that I'd assumed was some sort of closet or storage space, but when she opened the door, there was a good-sized room that had been converted into a bedroom.

The space itself wasn't girly, but there were touches that made it feel feminine, like the fresh flowers in the vase by the bed, a pretty eyelet bedspread, and a vanity on the left side of the bed. There was also a small sitting area, with a chair, ottoman, and end table, and my guitar case was propped up next to it.

I also noticed Dixie's pillow on the bed, and when I opened the closet, my clothes were hung, and my suitcases were on the floor.

"What do you think?" Ashley asked, nervously.

"I'm totally floored," I admitted. "I just assumed I'd be staying in one of the dorm rooms in the compound.

"Enzo wanted you to have your own space but still be close, so he came up with this. We made it neutral enough so his dad or brother or whomever could use it after you go back to Nashville. But he wanted you to feel comfortable while you're here."

I ran my hand over the comforter and tried to hide my emotions. I was truly touched and shocked that Enzo had cared enough to do this for me.

"You did terrific work. This will convert easily," I told her with a smile once I had control.

"I'm so happy you like it," she said happily. "Getting to work with you so closely has been a dream, and I was thrilled when Enzo asked me to help with this."

"I love it."

We went back into the living room to see the guys hauling heavy furniture up the stairs into the loft.

Ashley said she had to get going so we said goodbye and agreed to meet up for lunch one day soon.

Once alone, I looked around the space, taking it all in and really loving the way everything had come together. I went into the kitchen to see if there was water in the fridge and paused when I saw the setup of the liquor cabinet against the far wall by the breakfast nook.

There were glasses, an ice container, and a few decanters, as well as liquor, of course. But what drew my attention were the bottles of *Aplós* and *The Pathfinder*.

"Hey," I heard Enzo say, and looked over my shoulder to see him standing a few feet behind me.

"What made you get these?" I asked, gesturing at the bottles.

Enzo looked a little embarrassed and called back, "I'll be right out," to Tank, who nodded and walked out of the apartment.

He closed the distance between us and said, "Those were the drinks you asked for at Pony Up that night, right?" I nodded and he continued, "I thought it would be nice for us to enjoy a celebratory drink and figured it would be a safe bet getting those, rather than trying to pick something out at the market."

Neither beverage was available anywhere but online, so I knew he'd had to have gone searching and then had them shipped.

"That's really thoughtful of you, thank you," I said sincerely. "And thanks for the room. It all really means a lot."

I stepped in closer, as if pulled by some invisible force, suddenly eager to take him in my arms and hold him close.

I moved gingerly, waiting for any indication of a protest, and when I didn't get one, I encircled his waist and gave him a tight hug.

I'd always been told I was a good hugger, and I hoped he understood how grateful I was.

He smelled wonderful, like leather and spice, and I found my body responding to the scent and warmth of him surrounding me.

Tilting my head back, I looked up at him, eyes soft and lips feeling full and tender as I held my breath.

Enzo's eyes darted to my lips, then to my eyes, and his head dipped oh so slowly.

My eyes drifted shut and my heart began to pound in anticipation.

One second, I was waiting for the warmth of his lips on mine, and the next I was standing alone, feeling the chill of rejection.

I opened my eyes and crossed my arms over my chest when I saw him standing a few feet away, looking at me with regret.

"We can't," he said simply, then turned on his heel and walked out to join Tank and the others, leaving me there staring after him, wondering how I'd gotten things so wrong.

THIRTEEN

ENZO

Stepping back from Melody had been the hardest thing I'd ever done.

Standing there, looking so soft and pretty with her eyes closed, trusting, waiting for me to claim her lips.

I'd wanted to kiss her. Oh, so badly, but years of discipline and training had me holding back. Getting involved with a client went against everything my company stood for. And it would be quite hypocritical of me to give into the temptation myself yet hold my team to a different standard.

As tempting as it was, and as much as she'd taken over my thoughts lately, I knew I would regret it if I did, and the last thing I wanted to do was regret anything that happened between me and Melody.

I found myself really enjoying her company... hanging out together, listening to her sing through the walls, and the way she interacted with my dad. She was endearing, and much more than the country starlet I'd seen coming off the airplane that day.

I loved hearing her laugh, and the way she babied her little rat showed how much love she had in her heart.

If I was honest with myself, the only thing holding me back was the fact that I was hired to keep her safe. If we'd met under any other circumstances, there is no way I would have walked away without making her mine.

Unfortunately, that wasn't the case, so I needed to push my feelings aside and focus on the mission.

With that thought firmly in place, I headed down the stairs to the kitchen intent on making food.

And as if I'd conjured her, there was Melody, wearing short cutoffs and a frilly tank top, standing in front of the stove, her forehead burrowed in concentration. When she heard my feet hit the steps, she looked up and gave me an unsure smile.

"Hey. I, uh, thought I'd try making us some lunch," she said, her tone conveying her nerves. "I'm kind of embarrassed to say the only thing I really know how to make is grilled cheese, so that's what's on the menu. I didn't realize how much I'd come to rely on my chef, and restaurants."

"I love grilled cheese," I assured her. Honestly, there wasn't much I wouldn't eat. Once you've had to live off MREs, the packaged *meals ready to eat* that were given to us when we were in the field, any "real" food was a luxury.

"I may have burnt it a bit," Melody admitted, her cheeks flushed.

I chuckled and said, "Well-done works for me."

She plated the sandwiches and we walked over to the breakfast nook to eat.

"You've been so kind and thoughtful, I wanted to do something to give back," she said, picking up one triangle and laughing when she turned it over to reveal the black edges. "Guess I should have bought you a watch or something instead."

"Nah," I replied, taking a big bite. "You know they say food is the way to a man's…"

I let my sentence trail off, but we both knew what I'd been about to say, and an awkward silence settled between us.

After a few beats, Melody cleared her throat and said, "Uh, Tucker called me earlier. He invited me over tonight for dinner to meet his wife Justine, his son Matthew and Matthew's girl, Hannah. I guess Hannah's got a pretty brilliant voice and is interested in a career in country music, so he'd like me to meet with her. He also said you're more than welcome to come too, but I told him I'm not sure what your plans are."

I'd heard from Smith a couple days ago. Her stalker was still safely behind bars and so far, it looked like her location was still unknown in Nashville. Plus, I knew Tucker and Justine and knew she'd be completely safe and taken care of at their place.

Still, Smith had mentioned that Melody was still receiving letters, so he wasn't comfortable having her come back yet. I thought it best to remain diligent just in case Simon wasn't the only stalker she needed to be worried about.

Thinking of last night and the visions that had been going through my head since, I thought it may be good for us to spend a little time apart, even if it was only one evening.

I needed to get out and remind myself who I was and what my focus needed to be, so I looked at her and said, "I won't be able to make it, but I have no problem with you going... With the stipulation that Tank drives you, waits outside to keep watch, and then brings you home."

"Do you think that's necessary?" she asked.

"I do."

"Do you think he'll mind?"

I shook my head and said, "It's the job. Plus, he's just got here, so shouldn't have any other plans. I'll double check with him, and if he's not available, I'll get someone else, but I don't foresee any issues."

Melody nodded. "Okay, thanks."

I took another bite of the sandwich and said, "This is really good."

She looked pleased by my praise, which made me feel good. Once we were both done, I took the plates, rinsed them and put them in the dishwasher.

When I saw her standing near the counter, I told her, "I'll get with Tank now and let him know about tonight. What time do you want him ready?"

"Dinner's at six, so if we can leave like ten minutes beforehand. I know everything is pretty close here, and there's not usually traffic to deal with."

"One of the positives of small-town living."

She nodded and tucked her hair behind her ear.

"When would you like to go look at kittens?"

I pondered her question for a moment, then said, "I was thinking we'd go by there tomorrow, since we're going to see Pops in the evening. We can surprise him then."

Melody gave me an excited smile, which made my stomach do funny things, and said, "Awesome. I can't wait."

We parted ways, her heading toward her room, and me to my office to find Tank.

There was a dull ache in my chest at the thought of not spending the evening with her, which was exactly why we needed a little space.

FOURTEEN

MELODY

"Thanks again for bringing me," I told Tank as we pulled up in front of Tucker's house. "Are you sure you don't want to come inside and join us?"

Since Enzo had been included in the invitation, I didn't think Tucker would mind if Tank took his place.

"No, really, I'll be fine," Tank said with an easy grin. "I do this sort of thing all the time, and I've got my audiobook."

He held up his phone to show the audio cover of *Where the Crawdads Sing* as proof.

"Oh, I've been wanting to read that. How is it?" I asked, a little surprised by his reading choice.

"Great so far. A bit sad. But see, you don't have to worry about me. I'll be quite entertained. And on alert, so you don't need to worry about that either."

"I'm not," I replied honestly. "And I do appreciate you being here."

"Have a nice time," Tank said, so I opened the door to head inside and leave him to his book.

As I walked to the front door, I smoothed down my dress and fluffed out my hair a little. I wasn't in full glam mode, but still, old habits die hard.

I knocked and a few beats later, Tucker opened the door with a friendly smile.

"Hey, glad you could make it. Come on in," he said, stepping aside to give me room to walk past him.

"You have a lovely home," I said automatically. I'd been groomed by my mother in etiquette from a very young age.

Tucker shut the door, but before we could go farther into the house, the living room was suddenly filled with three more people. The first I knew was Justine, because she was a pretty brunette, just as he'd described, and her hand was resting protectively on her baby bump. The handsome young man, who was his doppelganger, but without the beard, would be Matthew, and the pretty young brunette next to him, whose mouth was currently gaping open had to be Hannah.

Since Tucker had asked me to come to meet her specifically, I focused on her first.

"You must be Hannah Murphy," I said in greeting.

Her eyes darted around the room before landing on me. "Melody Miles?"

I laughed at her exuberance and said, "In the flesh."

"But... *why are you here*? In Mason Creek?" she stuttered, and I could completely understand her shock. I remembered the first time I met Carrie Underwood. I'd barely been able to form words.

Tucker chuckled and said, "You know the Fratellis? Enzo is her heard of security and they thought Mason

Creek would be a good place for her to unwind and take a break from the spotlight for a bit."

"Well, you came to the right sleepy town for that," Hannah quipped.

"You must be Justine," I said, crossing to hand her the bouquet of flowers Tank and I had stopped to get on the way. "It's so nice to finally meet you. Tucker talks about you all the time."

"These are lovely," Justine said as she sniffed the flowers. "It's so good to meet you, too."

"And this is Matthew," Tucker said, gesturing to his son.

"Ah, yes, the baseball star."

We shook hands and then Tucker led us all into the dining room, where the table was already set for dinner. Family style.

"Can I get you something to drink?" Matthew asked as I started to take my seat.

"Water would be great," I replied.

Once we were all settled and dishes were being passed around the table, I looked over at Hannah and said, "So, Tucker and I were working on a song the other day and he told me all about you."

"He did?" she asked, looking between us with wide eyes.

Tucker chuckled and said, "Yes, I did. Don't sound so surprised."

"Sorry, but, *um*, it's *Melody Miles*!" she cried, then turned to me and admitted, "I'm still a little weirded out right now that we're sitting with you."

"Don't be," I said, placing my hand on the table. "I

was just like you only a few years ago trying to find my way into the music business."

"And look at you now," she said in awe.

I grinned. "*Look at me now*... But don't think it didn't take years of hard work. There were a lot of shows I played where I was a nobody. And it sounds like you're already making quite the name for yourself."

"Yeah, up here, away from anybody who really matters. I feel like I need to move to Nashville if I really want to go for it."

"Nashville definitely helps but what you're doing is good. Building a name for yourself here, so when you go to book gigs they can call back for a reference. Having people vouch for you will help get you booked faster."

Hannah tilted her head. "I never thought about it like that."

"Yep. Start collecting those contacts, girl. No matter how big or small you never know who you might need to call a favor on some day." I looked to Tucker and added, "Plus you got the best songwriter in the business sitting right here."

Tucker raised his eyebrows. "Yeah, but I only know that side of it. That's where I thought you could come in."

"Sure, I can introduce Hannah to the right people," I assured him, then brought my attention back to her and said, "I've heard your voice is pure magic. If so, all you'll need is an introduction. Your voice will do the rest."

"Are you being serious right now?" she asked, slapping the table excitedly.

"Sweetheart, if Tucker says you're good then I'm in.

Us girls need to stick together in the country music world."

She wiggled excitedly in her seat as Matthew wrapped his arms around her and gave her a hug. "I know you'll be someone someday. I just know it," he whispered sweetly.

And I couldn't help but wonder what a move to Nashville would do to their relationship. Young love was sweet, but if Hannah wanted to focus on building a career, it would be difficult to do if her attention was divided.

This train of thought made me think of me and Enzo and that almost kiss.

I was disappointed when he pulled away but knew a romantic entanglement between us would complicate things. Plus, we lived in completely different worlds, and not just physically. I was at the point in my life where casual relationships were no longer enough, but was Enzo the kind of man I could see myself with long term?

My heart was leaning that way, but my mind wasn't quite sure.

FIFTEEN

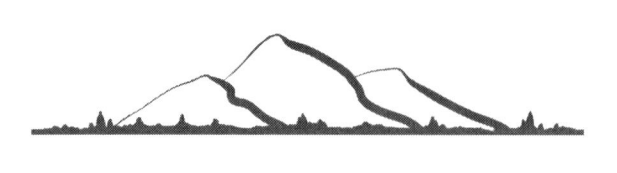

ENZO

"I'm so excited to see the kitties," Melody cooed as I parked my truck outside of the Mason Creek Rescue Shelter and Sanctuary.

I'd called earlier and had been told they'd recently rescued a new litter of kittens who were ready to be adopted.

"I wish Dixie could have come," Melody continued. "I know she would have loved seeing all the fur babies, but I understand that her prancing around and being a pup who already has a home wouldn't be fair to the other animals. Oh, how am I gonna get out of there without taking everyone home."

"Don't worry, I won't let you adopt anything," I assured her. The last thing I needed was my new place overrun with living things that tore stuff up and weren't trained. Dixie was already more than enough.

"Oh, don't be a grump," she joked as we started inside. "I know you have a soft spot in there somewhere, and I bet a sweet little kitten will be what brings it out."

"If you say so," I grumbled as I held the door open for her.

"Well hold me down and tickle me 'til I tinkle, if it isn't Lorenzo Fratelli walking through my doors. Come to whisk me away and save me from all this?"

The voice and phrasing had my head swinging toward a beautiful woman with a big, welcoming smile, long chestnut hair, and the most colorful outfit I'd ever seen. Now I knew that voice, but the woman looked nothing like the tomboy she used to be.

"Tate?" I asked, not completely sure I was right.

"You know it," she said, coming around the counter with her arms spread wide. "Now come lift me up and give me the biggest hug of your life, ya big lug."

I couldn't help but laugh as she threw herself into my arms. Now wanting to drop her, I held her back and swung her around for good measure. The laughter that had been the soundtrack of my childhood filled the room.

When I set her back on her feet, she slapped my arm jovially and gave Melody a curious look.

"I can't believe this is my first time seeing you since you came back to town," Tate said, placing her hands on her hips.

"Honestly, I had no idea you worked here," I admitted, feeling immediately guilty because I hadn't thought of her once since I left Mason Creek.

Tate had been Gino's best friend growing up. They'd been thick as thieves and had done everything together. I'd tolerated their presence, the way an older brother does, but I'd never actively hung out with them or anything.

"Sorry," I said, when I felt Melody's elbow dig into my side. "This is my brother Gino's friend, Tate. Tate, this is Melody."

"It's so nice to meet you, and it's Tatum," Tate said, holding out her hand. "I've gone by Tatum since graduation.

She gave me a wry glance and I simply shrugged, cause, *how the hell would I have known that?*

"Hi, Tatum," Melody replied, her expressing looking suspiciously happier now that she knew Tate was Gino's friend and not an old girlfriend like she'd probably assumed.

I had to admit, she *was* my type, but I'd never do that to Gino. I'd always thought he'd been secretly in love with Tate.

"It was you who called about the kittens, right? I thought I recognized your voice," Tate said, making me feel even more guilty, because I hadn't recognized hers at all.

"Yes, we can't wait to see them," Melody said, answering for me.

"Right this way," Tate said, taking us into the back. "Is this for the two of you?"

"Huh?" I asked, confused, then I understood that she thought Melody and I were together. "No, it's not like that... it's for Pops."

Tate shot me a familiar grin and said, "That's wonderful. A kitten will be great for Pops. I haven't seen him in a few weeks. How's he doing?"

"Better," I replied. Tate had been a fixture around our house when we were all kids, so Pops was like another father to her. "He's got a nurse who comes in to help out and I've got him eating better."

"Good," she said with a nod. "And one of these guys is sure to keep him mobile," she added as she opened a glass door and urged us inside.

The room was filled with cats. Cats on sofas, cats on those towers they scratched, cats sitting on the windowsill looking outside. Some were just kittens, while others were older. I don't know what I'd expected, but it wasn't this.

"There are so many of them," Melody said, her tone no longer excited.

"Yeah, even though we have a mobile spay/neuter van and urge people to keep their pets indoors, there are still too many abandoned animals out there procreating."

"Is there anything I can do? Any help you need? I'm assuming you're a nonprofit," Melody asked.

"Yes. And we always accept donations of any kind... food, toys, litter, and money, of course. But also, volunteers. We are going to have a booth at the Memorial Day Festival to try and get some pets adopted out. We do those types of events a few times a year."

I could see Melody's mind spinning with the possibilities.

"Which kittens are available for adoption today?" I asked, hoping to get back on track.

"Those over there, all cuddled together on the bed," she said, pointing to the group of kittens in the corner.

Melody walked over, crouched down, and started laughing when the kittens ambled over to her and rubbed against her legs. She ooed and ahhed over them for a while, petting each of them, before picking up a gray striped one.

He blinked sleepily at me and yawned big, showing off his teeth, before closing his eyes again.

"That one?" I asked, moving to Melody, and reaching out to scratch behind his ears.

She beamed at me and nodded.

"We'll take this one," I told Tate.

"Are you sure?" Tate asked. "You can take your time."

"Nope," I said, shaking my head definitively. "This one looks good. Shots up to date and everything?"

"They're current, but you'll want to make an appointment with Maria to get him checked and schedule upcoming shots. I'll give you a folder with all the information you need," she assured me as we walked back out to the front.

"Okay, thanks," I replied, eager to get everything done and head out.

"Do you have a card?" Melody asked. "I'd love to contact you once I figure out the best way I can help."

"Sure," Tate said, picking one up off the desk and handing it to her. "We'll just get all the paperwork done and you guys can be on your way." *Perfect*.

SIXTEEN

MELODY

I kept the kitten on my lap and stayed with him while Enzo ran into the store to get the supplies his dad would need for the cat. It was really adorable how focused he was on doing this for his father. And when he came out, loaded down with food, litter, a litter box, toys, treats, and dishes, I couldn't help but beam at him.

"What?" he asked as he pulled out of the lot and turned down the street toward his childhood home.

"Nothing. I just think it's very sweet of you to do this for Mario. I think he'll be pleasantly surprised," I said as I stroked the kitty's fur.

"I hope so," Enzo said dryly. "Because if not I'd have to find something else to do with this cat."

"You wouldn't keep him?"

"What would I do with a kitten?" he asked, looking truly puzzled.

"He could be, like, your office mascot or something," I suggested, then looked at him quizzically and asked, "Haven't you ever had a pet?"

"Uh, no. My mom was allergic, and then after she died there was a period of sadness where an animal actually probably would have helped a lot but didn't happen. As time went on, Gino and I got involved in school stuff and Pops was just doing everything he could to keep food on the table, so it never made sense."

"*Oh*," I muttered, thinking that sounded incredibly sad and how much I would have loved to get those grieving boys a puppy to love.

"I guess that's why it never even occurred to me to get a pet for my dad until I saw the way he was with Dixie. She really brought out a side of him I hadn't seen in years, and I'm hoping this cat will do the same. He deserves some happiness, you know?" Enzo said with a lift of his shoulders.

Unsure of how to broach the subject other than just spitting it out, I asked, "Did your father ever date again?"

Enzo started laughing. Like deep, belly laughter that turned almost manic as it went on.

As he parked in his dad's driveway, he started to calm and acted like he was wiping a tear from his eye.

"I guess that means no," I stated wryly.

He turned off the truck, took off his seatbelt, and shifted in his seat so he was looking at me.

"Look... my ma and Pops had the kind of relationship that comes along once in a lifetime. They made each other laugh, they danced in the kitchen, and they went to bed each night holding hands. The way he looked at her said it all. When she was gone, he was a shell of the man he'd been with her. He's gotten better over the years, for me and Gino, but he's never so much as looked at another woman as anything more than a friend. I don't think he can."

"That's amazing, but also, *really sad*," I said, hating the fact that Mario would spend so much more time without her than he had with her.

"I guess on one hand it is, but on the other? He got to be with the love of his life for sixteen years. That's a beautiful thing."

I nodded, because it was true, but my heart still felt heavy for him. For all of them.

"I guess that's why I've never been really serious with anyone. Because if what I feel for them isn't *that*... then what's the point. I'm not going to waste my time and energy for a temporary thing. I want the real deal or nothing."

"Wow, that's really... self-aware." When his face changed, I realized he thought I was making fun of him. "No, I'm serious. Most people aren't that in tune with what they really want out of a relationship, and out of life. But you had the perfect example of what you want, and I think it's amazing that you aren't willing to compromise. It's commendable, Enzo, truly."

The kitten shifted and let out a mew.

"Let's get him inside," Enzo said, putting his hand on the door handle. "Pop's is probably watching from the window and wondering what's taking so long."

I probably looked silly, but as I got out, I tried to tuck the kitten under my shirt, just in case his dad *was* watching from the window. I didn't want to ruin the surprise.

Enzo grabbed the bags and I followed him up to the

door. When he put his hand out to open the door, Mario beat him to it and the door swung open.

"Whatchya got there?" Mario asked him.

"If you'd let us in, we'll show you," Enzo said with a grunt as he moved past Mario into the house.

As I stepped in after him, I pulled the kitten out from under my shirt and held him up so Mario could get a good look at him.

"Dad, this little guy is for you," Enzo said as he started taking items out of bags and placing them on the coffee table and couch.

"What?" Mario's eyes widened in shock as he reached out to take the sweet baby from my hands.

He held him up to look into his face, before cradling him to his chest.

"Enzo saw how much you liked hanging out with Dixie," I began.

"I thought you might like a little companion," Enzo said, stepping next to his dad and reaching out to scratch the kitten behind his ear. "His shots are up to date, but we'll make an appointment with the vet to get him all checked out. I think I got everything you'll need to start, and if you tell me where you'll want his litter box and food bowls, I can get them set up."

"Uh... litter box in the laundry room and bowls in the kitchen?"

"That works," Enzo said, and moved to get things done.

"What do you think?" I asked, moving closer so I could pet the kitten. "Do you love him?"

"He's very cute," Mario said, his face showing his pleasure.

"What do you think you'll name him?" I asked, because, honestly, that's all I'd been thinking about since Enzo picked him from the litter.

Mario lifted him to look into his face again and said, "Rocky."

SEVENTEEN

ENZO

"Dang it, I knew I should've bet you on what he'd name the cat," I grumbled as I finished plating the fish, steamed broccoli, and brown rice. "I knew *for a fact* my dad would pick Rocky. It's his favorite movie of all time."

"It *is* a great movie and I think the name suits him," Melody said as she took the plates to the table.

Rocky was currently wide awake and playing with the string on a rope toy I'd bought him, while Pops laughed happily at his new pet.

"It's a classic," I agreed as I grabbed a beer for me and my dad and a glass of water for Melody. "Dad, let's eat," I called out, and my dad reluctantly left the cat and sat down at the table.

"What kind of fish is this?" he asked, his eyes on Rocky who was prancing around the kitchen floor.

"Salmon," I replied.

"I bet you like salmon," Pops cooed to Rocky who'd found his way to the table.

"I'm sure he does, but he's just a baby, it's probably not good for him."

My dad glanced at me and asked, "You think?"

I shrugged. "How do I know. We'll ask the vet when we take him. Til then, I'd err on the side of caution."

Pops bobbed his head in agreement and whispered, "*Sorry, Rock.*"

Melody bit back a giggle and dug into her food.

"Have you heard from Gino?" I asked my dad, taking a swing of beer.

"Yeah. Looks like he'll be here soon. Right after the festival."

"Is this the same festival Tate mentioned? For Memorial Day?" Melody asked excitedly, practically bouncing in her chair.

"One and the same," I replied.

"You met Tate?" Pops asked, his expression softening at the mention of Gino's childhood friend.

"Yes, we got Rocky from the animal rescue place," she replied.

"She's a peach, that one. I miss having her around the place. Maybe once Gino is back for good, she'll start coming around again."

"She's not quite the same as she was as a kid, Pops, and neither is Gino," I reminded him.

"Bah, she may be a young woman now, but she's still the same where it counts. And it would be good for Gino to find a little bit of who he used to be. He always sounds so miserable on the phone."

"I'm sure he'll be good."

"So, what happens at this festival?" Melody asked,

when there was a pause in conversation. "I love festivals. Big ones, small ones… they're always so much fun!"

"The usual stuff," I said. "Booths for food and games and such, live music, the auction."

"Auction?" she asked, intrigued.

"Usually, the single women make a nice picnic basket and the single men bid on it to share. It's all for a good cause and all in good fun," Pops said with a grin. "But this year things are going to be different."

"How so?" Melody asked.

"Well… and I've been meaning to bring this up with you, Enzo… but this year the organizers have decided to switch things up, and they want the single men to make the basket and get auctioned. In the name of equality, and all that."

"What does that have to do with me?" I asked my father with a frown.

"The changeup was actually Hattie and Hazel's idea and they asked for you specifically to be one of the men involved."

"To be auctioned?" I asked, horrified at the thought. "I never even go to this festival, let alone participate. Why do they think now's any different?"

"C'mon, it's for a good cause. Think of the children," my dad cajoled. "Plus, wouldn't it be nice to eat a nice lunch with a woman willing to pay to spend time with you?"

I shot him a death glare and said, "No."

"I can help you put together the basket," Melody offered, her expression hopeful.

I sighed and said, "You guys aren't gonna let this go, are you?"

Melody and my dad shook their heads in unison. It would have been funny if I wasn't so annoyed.

"Fine, here's the deal," I began, putting my elbows on the table and tenting my fingers. "I'll do it, but only if Tank, and *you*, do it too."

I pointed my hands at my dad who looked shocked.

"Me? I can't do that," Mario stuttered.

Crossing my arms over my chest, I sat back in the chair.

"So, you're more than happy to throw *me* to the wolves, but not get involved yourself?"

"I can't go on a date with someone else," Pops repeated, and although I knew where he was coming from, I thought it would be good for him to get out there and have new experiences too.

"Dad, it wouldn't be like that. It's not like an actual date where you're saying things are going to progress into a relationship. It's all in good fun," I said, then mimicked, *"Think of the children."*

"I'll bid on you, Mario, then you don't have to be worried," Melody promised.

I scowled at her and said, "That's cheating."

"I can bid on you, too," she amended with a suspiciously sweet smile.

"And Tank? You gonna buy his basket too?" I asked.

"Nah, I think it'll do good for him to meet someone here locally," she said. "Who knows, maybe it'll work out for him."

I grunted, but actually liked the idea.

Pops sighed dramatically, and said, "Okay if you'll bid on me, I'll do it."

"And I'll make Tank do it with me, so I guess I'm a *yes* too," I added.

"*Yay!*" she said, clapping her hands, "*This is going to be so much fun!*"

EIGHTEEN

MELODY

"Hey, Smith, how are things back home?" I asked as I hurried through town square.

I was helping Tatum out with her booth during the morning shift of the festival, so I'd asked Enzo to drop me off a little early.

"Everything's on track here, being taken care of. You don't need to worry or even give it a second thought. Chris Simon is scheduled to have a court appearance in the next two weeks, and I've already discussed it with the judge and it's totally fine for you to do your testimony via Zoom. Everyone has agreed that they don't want to subject you to being in the same room with him."

"Any more letters?" I asked, hoping he would say no, so we would know Chris Simon was the only person I needed to worry about.

"Not since the one I told you about last week."

"Wow, that's such a relief. Thank you so much. And thanks for holding down the fort there and setting me up here with Enzo. I don't know what I'd do without you."

"You can count on me, you know that," he replied easily, and it was true, I did know that. Smith had been the one constant in my Nashville career.

I was lucky to have him.

"You won't believe where I am," I gushed.

"Where?"

"A festival. It's the Mason Creek Memorial Day Festival and it's just as cute as can be. All decorated, with the smell of funnel cake already filling the air. I'm going to help out with an animal rescue booth, then there's a charity auction, and Tucker called last night and asked me to do a couple songs with him."

"Aren't you supposed to be keeping a low profile?" he asked, his tone worried.

"I am, but there's nothing to fear here, I promise. It's the smallest of small towns. Everyone knows everyone, and if there were an unfamiliar face, they'd say something. Plus, Tucker and I want to try out the new song we wrote."

"I can't wait to hear it. You be safe now, ya hear?"

"I promise. Talk soon."

"All right. Have a good day, Melody."

I hung up just as I saw Tatum's booth and went rushing over.

"Good morning," I called as I approached.

Tatum's head swung up and she shot me a big grin.

"Morning, Melody Miles... I can't believe Enzo didn't say anything about who you were. I mean, I knew you looked familiar, but I just never would have guessed."

"It's no big deal," I assured her, hoping it wouldn't be. I wanted to help out today, but I didn't want to make her feel uncomfortable, which my celebrity status did sometimes.

"Well, sure it is," she said, pulling her long hair off of her neck and piling it on top of her head. "My last breakup, I must have listened to *You Left Me Stranded* on repeat."

You Left Me Stranded was my first big hit.

"I still cry when I sing that one sometimes," I admitted.

"Sorry, come on back," Tatum said when she realized I was still standing outside the booth.

I rounded the table and went back to where she had a gated area for the puppies set up. They were currently still in cages. Some sleeping, some eating, and one gnawing on the metal that was holding it in.

"You can help me take them out and put them in the pen. We'll rotate them, because believe it or not they usually sleep better in the kennel, since we work on crate training them as soon as they come into the rescue."

"Okay," I said enthusiastically, then moved to open the door to the puppy who was on a mission to chew his way to freedom. "Hey buddy," I cooed as I held him close. "Aren't you a sweetheart."

I placed him on the grass, and he immediately started running around and playing with the dog Tatum had just put in.

"*Oh my gosh*, how do you not adopt them all yourself?" I asked, my heart hurting at the thought of them not having a home.

Tatum laughed and said, "It was really hard at first. I love animals, which is why I do what I do, but I also find great satisfaction in finding them each a loving home with a family, or person, who needs them just as much."

"That must feel great."

"It does, but you know how that feels... to do something that matters."

I thought about the people, like Tatum, who relayed to me the ways my songs had touched them, or helped them, or even simply made them happy, and I nodded. "Yeah, I do, and there's nothing like it in the world."

We finished putting the first round of dogs in the pen, and I swear, I fell in love with each one a little more than the one before. Then I felt guilty thinking about Dixie back at Enzo's and how mad at me she was going to be when she smelled all of these dogs on me when I got back.

"I hope all of you get adopted today," I told them.

"That's the goal," Tatum said. "And here comes the first prospect."

Pretty soon we were overrun by people.

Kids wanting to pet the puppies, people who were curious but didn't want to commit, and those who stopped by, fell instantly in love, and left with a new family member.

By the time my shift was over, eight puppies and two older dogs had been adopted, and I was over the moon about it.

"Thanks so much for helping out," Tatum said.

"It was my pleasure. I'm about to grab a grilled cheese and then find a spot by the gazebo for the auction. Are you coming?" I asked.

"I'll stop by if I get a chance. If nothing else, it should

at least be good for a laugh. I can't believe you talked Enzo into doing it. He's going to hate every second."

I laughed and said, "I know," then said my goodbyes to the remaining animals before telling Tatum and her crew, "See you guys later."

NINETEEN

ENZO

I've done a lot of stupid things over the years, but I've never felt as foolish as I do now.

"Thanks for doing this, Lorenzo," Hattie, one of the *Twisted Sisters*, said from behind me.

I turned and looked down at her. "I feel like an idiot." I lifted the basket Melody had made for me as evidence.

Hattie clucked her tongue at me and said, "Nonsense. It's for the children, and I have a feeling you're going to raise a lot of money."

I snorted and said, "Don't get your hopes up."

I could hear Judge Nelson, who was the emcee, out front getting the crowd pumped up, and from the sound of it, the entire town was out there waiting to watch the first *male* auction of Mason Creek.

I turned to thank my dad *once more* for dragging me into this, but when I saw the look on his face, I stopped.

He looks terrified.

"Pops," I called softly as I moved toward him. "You good?"

"This was a bad idea," he said, his eyes swiveling back and forth. "I don't want to do it."

I placed my hands on his shoulders and said, "You're overthinking it. Everything is gonna be fine. The judge will announce you; you'll step out for a few moments while he does his little soundbite and then Melody will bid on you and it'll be over. But, if you really don't want to go through with this, you don't have to. We can call Hattie over and tell her."

My dad took a deep breath and shook his head. "No, it's for a good cause. I can do this. It's only a few minutes of my life, right?"

"Right." *A few horrible, excruciating minutes.*

"Lorenzo, you're up first," Hattie called.

"Great," I muttered, then told my dad, "See you after."

I moved toward the stage, like a lamb to slaughter, and reminded myself that going first meant it would be over quicker and I could relax with what was actually a pretty decent meal. Since Melody made it, and knew we'd be the ones eating it, she'd tailored the basket specifically toward us.

When I got to the curtain, I paused, and Hattie practically shoved me out onto the stage. I turned back to scowl at her, but she simply smiled and waved her fingers at me.

"Here he is now, *Lorenzo Fratelli*," Judge Nelson announced, raising his arm to beckon me over to him. "Lorenzo is a homegrown boy who left us to serve this great nation of ours and has come back as the CEO of his very own business. *Ladies...* he's single, has a good job, and comes from a good family. Don't let this one pass you by. We'll start the bidding at fifty dollars."

Only the judge could get away with calling me a boy, I thought as I looked out over the crowd.

I saw some of the guys I'd gone to school with, Blake, Aiden, Mitch, and Grady, as well as Tucker. Of course, they were all in happy relationships, so none of them were subjected to being up on this stage.

I vaguely heard the judge call out, "Do I hear five hundred," but it didn't really register until I noticed the paddles being raised as women bid. Women of all ages. Some I'd known all my life, with a few new faces scattered in, but when I found Melody in the crowd, I focused on her.

She was biting her lip and intensely watching the other bidders, often scowling when they raised their paddles.

I bit back a laugh at how serious she was taking this, and then I lost all humor when I heard him call out, "One thousand," and saw Melody's paddle swing up.

A thousand? That's too much. She shouldn't waste that kind of money on me.

I was about to get her attention and signal for her to stop bidding when the Judge said, "S*old*, for one thousand dollars to the beautiful redhead in the back."

Melody jumped up and started clapping with her paddle still in her hand, like she actually won, rather than simply going through with the plan we'd had in place all along.

Judge Nelson indicated I should exit the stage and go join my winner. Happy it was over, I hurried down the steps and through the crowd to Melody, pausing to say hi and accept congratulations from people I knew.

Although why they were congratulating me was a mystery, I hadn't done anything more than sell myself off like cattle.

When I reached Melody, she cried, "*I won!*"

"*I know,*" I replied with a chuckle. "Let's get away from here for a minute."

Once we were far enough away from the crowd, I took a deep breath and let it out.

"That was intense," I said, looking back toward the stage in time to see Tank saunter out like he was born for the spotlight.

"It was kind of a rush," Melody said, somewhat breathless. "I never realized how exciting auctions were. I can see how people become addicted."

"I appreciate you doing that. I don't know what I would have done if you weren't here," I admitted.

Melody moved a little closer, a smile playing on her lips as she looked up at me.

"Oh, I'm sure you would have managed. Did you see how beautiful some of those women who were bidding on you are?"

I gravitated toward her and said honestly, "I didn't notice anyone else."

"*Oh,*" she whispered, her mouth dropping open slightly. Her hands drifted toward my waist, and I moved the basket to the side as she grasped my shirt gently.

My head started to dip down, as if there were a magnetic pull bringing closer, and I saw desire in her eyes that I knew matched my own.

I wasn't thinking about professionalism or rules; my only thoughts were of Melody, and how her lips would feel against mine. How she'd taste. What sounds she'd make when I brought her pleasure.

Seconds before closing the gap between us, I heard the judge say, "Come on, ladies, you know you've been waiting to sit down for a meal with Mario Fratelli."

Melody must have heard it too, because she jumped back and cried, "Oh no, I'm supposed to bid on your dad."

TWENTY

MELODY

I took off running back toward the auction. I could see Mario's head swerving back and forth, and although I couldn't see his face, I knew he was looking for me and was probably mid-panic because I wasn't there.

Enzo was right beside me and when I glanced over at him, I could see the guilt I was feeling reflected on his face.

Just then, I saw the judge hit the gavel and knew Mario's basket had sold.

"Shoot," I gasped as I stopped to catch my breath, bending at the waist, and putting my hands on my knees as I scanned the crowd. "Do you see who got it? Maybe I can make them a better offer and buy it back."

Enzo's face cleared and he grinned.

"We're good," he said, and I followed his pointed finger to see Tatum walking toward the stage waving her paddle. "Tate got him."

"*Oh, thank God!*" I exclaimed, then grimaced and

said, "Mario's still gonna kill me though. I broke my promise. He must have been freaking out."

"Come on, let's go check on him."

We moved through the crush of people to the other side where Tatum and Mario had stopped.

When we reached them, I hurried to Mario and threw my arms around him.

"I'm so sorry. I can't believe I missed it... but Enzo and I had walked away, and I didn't realize Tank would be done so fast and that you were after him. I have no excuse. I broke my promise," I cried, holding him tight.

"Don't be so hard on yourself," Mario said reassuringly. "I did have a moment of panic when I didn't see you, but then Tate came to my rescue."

"I walked up just in time to see Mario on stage looking like he was about to pass out, and I swear, every single woman over the age of forty was about to get in a rumble vying for this man's picnic basket. He's a hot commodity."

I glanced around and noticed a few upset glances in our direction.

"Looks like we opened pandora's box," I muttered.

"That box needs to remain firmly closed," Mario insisted. "This is part of the reason I didn't want to participate. The last thing I need is for people to think I'm on the market. That part of my life is over."

My first instinct was to argue and say something like, *don't close yourself off to a chance at happiness* or *there still may be someone out there to share your life with.* Partially because I truly believed those things, and partially because we're trained to believe that people can't be happy unless they're spending their lives with someone else.

But as I looked at the dead-serious expression on Mario's face and thought about what Enzo told me about his parents, I realized it really wasn't up to me to have an opinion on someone else's happiness or relationship status.

So, I kept my mouth shut.

Mario had been with the love of his life and been very happy, and now that she was gone, he was content living out the rest of his life as a single man.

I could see how the local women would be excited though. Mario Fratelli was definitely a catch.

"What do you say we go enjoy our picnics together?" Tatum suggested.

"What about Tank? Did we see where he ended up? Maybe he wants to join us," I suggested.

Enzo surveyed the scene then grinned and said, "Nah, I think he's good where he is."

I followed his gaze to see Tank sitting under a large tree enjoying his meal with a beautiful woman, a huge smile on his face.

"Yeah, he seems *just* fine," I said wryly with a grin. "Let's go find someplace to eat, I'm starving."

We enjoyed a lovely lunch, and I had a great time walking around the festival, buying trinkets and handmade items, and snacking on way more junk than I usually allowed myself. By the time evening rolled around, I was exhausted, so when Tucker asked if I wanted to join him and Hannah on stage for a song, I said I could, but only the one.

We sang Little Big Town's *Pontoon* to a lively, dancing crowd, and Tucker was right. Hannah was magic up on that stage.

Enzo and I walked into his place, and I made a beeline for my room. "I'm going to get out of these clothes and into something comfortable."

"Want a drink?" he called out after me.

"Yes, please," I shouted back.

A few moments later I was in my pajamas and met Enzo in the kitchen.

He'd made me an *Aplós* with club soda and a blood orange slice, and a bourbon neat for himself.

"Thank you," I said, accepting the glass and taking a sip. "Are you going to bed, or do you want to watch a movie or something?"

"A movie sounds good. I like to unwind a bit before bed," he replied, and we journeyed to the couch.

I grabbed a throw blanket and sat next to Enzo on the couch, while he fired up his Neo QLED 8K TV. It was the most beautiful television I'd ever seen, with a picture so crisp and clear it was like you were there.

"Any preference?" Enzo asked.

"I'm good with anything."

He picked a Kevin Hart buddy comedy movie that I'd never seen before. I sipped on my drink and leaned back on the sofa laughing along as I got comfortable. I started dozing off and barely registered when Enzo took the glass from my hand. I drifted toward the warmth of his body, and promptly passed out.

TWENTY-ONE

ENZO

"*Now that's what I call strictly professional!*"

At first my brain registered an annoying buzzing sound, but eventually I came too enough to realize it was the sound of my brother's voice.

I opened one eye to find Gino standing in front of me, arms crossed, grinning like an idiot.

At first, I wondered what the hell he was doing in my room, then I took in my surroundings and remembered watching a movie with Melody and then nothing after that. As soon as that penetrated, so did the fact that the weight on top of me was not from my weighted blanket but was actually a pint-sized redhead.

"*Shit*," I muttered under my breath, trying not to register how her body felt against mine, especially with my brother watching, The last thing I needed to do was stand before him with a raging boner.

Gino chuckled as I did my best to disengage myself from Melody without waking her up. Good thing she slept like the dead, because I was able to ease out from under her and her only reaction was to snuggle deeper into the couch.

I covered her with the blanket and gestured to my brother to head out of my living space to give her some privacy.

Once we were out in the hall leading to my work area, I pulled him in for a hug and clapped him on the back. "It's good to see you, man. If you would have told me you were coming today, I'd have been up and ready for you."

"I wanted it to be a surprise," Gino said, then lifted his chin toward my door and grinned. "How's that going?"

"It's not what you think. We just fell asleep watching a movie. Nothing is going on between us," I said matter-of-factly, but I wasn't quite sure which one of us I was trying to convince, as flashes of the way her soft curves felt against me kept sneaking into my thoughts.

"Funny how you keep insisting that," Gino said with a smirk.

"You've been here literally five minutes," I argued, moving down the hall toward my office where I could make some coffee.

"I'm just sayin'... usually you either give me a dirty look or ignore my taunts all together, but with Melody you become *very* defensive. I'm simply saying I think it's interesting."

"You just got here and you're already getting on my nerves."

"That's what brothers are for," Gino said, undeterred.

"Tank and the guys are already up and out for a run. I passed them on the way in."

I grunted in response and started the pot.

"Want a cup?" I asked him as I grabbed a mug off a shelf.

"Sure."

I pulled down a second mug and got out the cream and sugar. I took my coffee black, but my brother liked to pollute his until it could barely pass as coffee.

"You already been home?" I asked while we waited.

Gino sat down in one of the chairs opposite my desk and said, "Yeah, I got in last night. I met Rocky and Pops told me all about how you made him do the auction at the festival. I can't believe you talked him into it."

"He was pressuring me to do it, so I made him a deal," I said with a shrug. "I knew it wouldn't mean anything, Lord knows he has no interest in dating, but I thought it would be good for him to get out and do something in the community. Ever since he got sick, he's been hanging around the house too much. It can't be good for him."

"He said Tate bought his basket," Gino commented with a smile that said he was remembering one of the million times they got into mischief as children.

"Have you seen her?" I asked, pouring coffee into his cup, and placing it before him, along with the cream and sugar.

As he defiled the coffee, he said, "No, not in over a decade. Every time I came home and tried to get in touch, she was either out of town or couldn't swing it. I always thought it was weird, but I can understand. We've grown up and moved on with our lives."

"Well, let me warn you, she *does not* look the same. *At all.*"

"How so?" he asked, curious.

"You know... she was always kind of gangly and awkward..."

"She was not," Gino protested.

I shot him a look that said, *she was*, then kept going as if he hadn't interrupted. "Well, now, she's beautiful. A real knockout."

"Who's a knockout?" Melody asked sleepily from the doorway.

I glanced over to see her standing there, looking deliciously rumpled and still half asleep.

"Tate," I answered, then amended, "Sorry, *Tatum*." I looked back at my brother. "That's another thing that's changed."

"Oh, yeah, she's gorgeous," Melody agreed, then whimpered, "I smelled coffee."

I chuckled and pulled down another cup. Once it was full, I crossed to her and said, "I don't have any oat milk in here."

"That's okay, I can go get some."

She finally noticed we weren't alone in the room and blinked rapidly a few times until Gino's presence sifted through her brain fog and her eyes widened.

"Gino?" she screeched, making my brother jump in his seat. "You're here!"

Melody moved so quickly, she sloshed coffee out of her cup and onto the floor, which caused me to curse and reach for some napkins, while Gino put his cup down and stood up to accept her welcome.

I grabbed the cup from her hand before she could do any more damage, just as she launched into his arms.

"I'm so happy to meet you," she gushed. "I feel like I already know you after staying in your room. Sorry about that, I hope you don't feel like I violated your personal space. Oh, and I know Mario is thrilled to have you back. And so is Enzo, although he's less likely to show it."

Gino laughed at her rapid-fire greeting and said, "I've been looking forward to meeting you too. In fact, I came over to see about taking you to Wren's for breakfast. *Both* of you."

"I'd love that," Melody said happily. "I'll go get ready."

She snatched her cup from my hands and twirled out of the room, leaving us alone once more.

"She's something," he said, eyeing me with a mischievous glint.

"Behave," I ordered, taking a long drink.

Gino held up his hand and said, "Scouts honor."

"You were never a Scout, and it's three fingers, not four."

TWENTY-TWO

MELODY

I got dressed as quickly as possible, worried they would leave without me and not wanting to miss a second.

It was funny seeing them together. Gino was like a smaller version of Enzo, in both size and stature. They had the same coloring and residual short military hair cut, but while Enzo was usually clean shaven, Gino's facial hair had already started to grow out.

I found them waiting for me in the open bay area talking to the guys who must have just gotten back from their run.

Gino was laughing at something Tank had said, while Enzo stood there shaking his head.

"Good morning," I called to the guys as I approached.

They all replied in kind and the Fratelli brothers and I left them to go to breakfast after they all declined an invitation to join us so they could shower and drink their morning protein shakes.

It was a quick trip to Wren's Café and since it was such a nice day, we all agreed on sitting outside. There was plenty of shade from the trees, so the early morning sun wouldn't get too hot, and I loved all the greenery surrounding the patio in wooden crates. It had a fun, rustic feel to it.

"I've been dying for Shorty's pancakes," Gino said as he picked up the menu.

"Oh, are they good?" I asked as I perused it myself. "I was thinking about the market hash and eggs."

"Yeah, it's all good. You really can't go wrong with any of it," he replied easily.

Enzo hadn't even picked up the menu, so I asked, "You already know what you want?"

"He always gets the same thing," Gino said with a grin. "Biscuits and gravy with two eggs over medium and a side of crispy bacon. With black coffee, of course."

"You never change it up?" I asked Enzo.

He gave a half shrug and said, "I know what I like."

His eyes seemed to change as he said it, and he didn't take them off of me. I shifted in my seat as my skin began to warm under his stare, and I couldn't help but think he was saying he saw something else he liked.

Gino made a choking sound, and when I looked back at him, he was covering his mouth with one hand and waved the other. "Sorry. I must have swallowed a bug or something."

Just then a server with *Amber* on her name tag came over and asked if she could get us started with anything.

"Can we get some water, please, he needs to clear his throat."

"He's fine," Enzo said. "I think we're ready to order."

Gino and I both nodded, confirming we were ready,

so Amber took our orders and promised to have our food out soon.

"So, Gino, tell me everything," I said, getting comfortable in my chair. "How did you like the Army? Did you enjoy living in South Carolina? Do you have a girlfriend? Are you happy to be back in Mason Creek?"

Gino laughed and glanced at his brother, who just said, "Yeah..."

"Okay, where to start?" Gino said, thanking Amber when she brought out our waters, coffee for me and Enzo and a large orange juice for him. "I am happy to be back home and can't wait to get settled and see everyone in town. I enjoyed the opportunities the Army gave me and plan to go to school online after I'm all up to speed on the job. South Carolina was nice, but a bit too humid sometimes. And although I have been lucky to have relationships with a few wonderful women, I am not currently attached to anyone. Did I get it all?"

I smiled at him, enjoying his candor and good humor.

"I believe you did, yes."

"Great. My turn."

I nodded, indicating he should go ahead and ask.

"How does a New Yorker end up singing country songs in Nashville?"

"Wow, good question," I said, pleasantly surprised at his forethought, and that he knew enough about me to know where I was from.

"I may have Googled you," he admitted sheepishly.

I laughed lightly and said, "That's okay. I'm sure you're curious about who's spending all this time with your family... So, *yes*, I *am* a New Yorker, and I grew up in a fancy building with a doorman and learned how to behave in nice restaurants by the age of three. And I'm sure you saw most of that on Google. My mom was born and bred in the city and comes from a family that goes back for generations there. My dad, however, is from a small town in Georgia."

Gino nodded. This was all common knowledge, at least the surface stuff.

"Well, in the summers he would take me back to his parents' farm and it was my absolute favorite place in the world. My grandpa would sit on the porch with his guitar in the evenings and we would sing together. Dolly Parton, Conway Twitty, and George Straight were some of his favorites. So, when I decided I wanted to sing for a living, I knew Nashville was the place for me. And the rest, as they say, is history."

"Your grandpa must have been really proud."

"Unfortunately, he passed away before I made it, but he did get to hear me sing in a few musicals in high school," I said, a feeling of sadness washing over me at the memories.

I felt a hand cover mine and looked up to see Enzo watching me, his eyes soft. "I'm sorry."

The sadness lifted and my heart warmed.

"Thank you," I said knowing he was coming from the place of someone who had lost someone very important to him.

Amber arrived with our food and the moment passed as Gino said, "Heck yeah, let's eat!"

TWENTY-THREE

ENZO

"Rise and shine," I called through Melody's door, giving two firm knocks before stepping back and waiting for a response.

"Hmphr," was what I heard.

"Get up, Princess. The boys and I have decided to spend the day at the lake."

I heard a thump and then the sound of something falling before the scrambling of feet and the door flew open.

"The lake?" Melody asked, her hair sticking up in all directions, Dixie under her arm.

I bit back a laugh and acted like I didn't notice anything.

"Yes, ma'am. So, grab a bathing suit and anything else you need. We're renting a boat and soaking up the sun."

"Yay," she cheered, doing some sort of dance shuffle with her feet that made me laugh. "I love the water."

"As do we all. The boys are packing and loading up

the trucks. Meet us out front when you're ready, yeah? Pops said he'll pick up Dixie."

I left her squealing behind me and found myself smiling all the way back outside.

There was something about her energy and overall positive vibe that I found really refreshing.

When we first met, I'd admit, I'd kind of stereotyped her as the usual rich, high-maintenance, attention-loving star that I was used to working with. But Melody wasn't like that at all. Sure, she liked the finer things in life, but I was pretty sure those were things she had grown accustomed to having since birth. She wasn't jaded, snooty, or rude. She was sweet, funny, and honestly made happy by the smallest things.

"I bet I know what put that smile on your face," Tank joked as I joined the guys.

I wiped the smile right off.

"Shut up."

He just smirked.

A couple of the guys were about to go out of town for a couple jobs we'd just taken on, so we thought it would be fun to spend a day kind of welcoming them to town, and subsequently sending them off to work.

In record time, Melody came flying down the hall, her long dress flowing behind her, sunglasses on her face, and beach bag in hand.

"Ready," she called as she came skidding to a halt next to us.

We all loaded up and headed out of town toward Baylor Lake, a fleet of big black trucks filled with a bunch of ex-military men and one Nashville superstar.

By the time we rented the boat and got ready to take it out, the sun was out in full force. There were six of us—me and Melody, Tank, and three of my other men Ty, Snape, and Cargo. We'd gotten a pontoon boat to accommodate everyone and because we really just wanted a nice relaxing day on the water.

The cooler was filled with beer and water, and we'd grabbed provisions from the Deli Sub Shop on our way out of town.

Once everything and everyone was on board, I started her up and navigated out into the open water. The cool breeze perfectly complemented the warm rays, and it didn't take long for the guys to strip off their shirts, pop beer cans, and find a spot to sprawl out.

What I wasn't prepared for, was turning around to see Melody shimmying out of her dress to reveal an emerald-green bikini underneath. The top showcased her assets perfectly, and when she turned, I saw it tied in the back with a bow.

I never wanted to unwrap something so badly in my life.

When she pulled out a bottle of suntan lotion and proceeded to rub it all over her exposed skin, I very purposefully turned my ass back around and focused on the course ahead.

I seriously didn't think this through, I chided myself, *It's going to be a very long day*.

I took us out to the spot my dad had always taken us on Baylor Lake. It was a little island. We'd drop anchor a little way out and then make our way to shore. It was deep, but Tank and I would be able to walk it with the lunch stuff. Melody would have to swim in.

"Okay, guys, from here, you can either head to the island and relax, eat, whatever, or from the back side of the boat, it's deep enough to jump off and swim out. We'll stay here for a while, so feel free to do whatever makes you happy. The day is ours," I said, then finally managed to look over at Melody, who was laying in the sun on the back deck of the boat. "I got you a veggie wrap, the guys'll take it to the beach with the rest of the food, unless you'd rather hang out here."

"I'll come over with everyone," she said, standing up and stretching before me.

Good Lord, she's trying to kill me.

"See you over there," Melody said with a sly grin, then turned and dove off.

"She's like a fish," Tank said from beside me. "A sparkling, sexy as hell, fish."

I shot him a look and asked, "Do you need something?"

"No, *boss*. Just making an observation," he replied with a grin, unperturbed by my ire.

"Then let's go," I said grumpily, ignoring the soft chuckle that followed me.

We all relaxed on the shore. Some snoozing, some eating, and Snape and Cargo tossing a football around.

"This was a great idea," Melody said, surprising me. She was laying out and her eyes had been closed for a while, so I'd thought she'd fallen asleep.

"Yeah, Tank gets good ones every once in a while," I joked.

He gave me the finger.

"It's too bad Gino couldn't come with us," she added.

"I asked him, but he and Pops already had plans. He said *next time*."

I saw her frown a little, and realized she was thinking she probably wouldn't be around next time.

I didn't want to think about how that realization made me feel.

It had only been a short period of time in the grand scheme of things, but Melody had quickly become a fixture in my daily life. I don't know how it happened, but she'd gotten under my skin, and I knew I'd miss her when she was gone.

TWENTY-FOUR

MELODY

By the time we got back home, my nerves were shot.

I mean, I lived with Enzo, so I knew how often he worked out, and obviously could see his biceps and how his shirts fit him like a glove. But I still hadn't been prepared for the visual impact of seeing him in only swim trunks.

His abs had abs.

The man was *fit*.

I'd never thought of myself as someone who was turned on by muscles. I'd fallen for a man's smile, his voice, or how kind he was to those around him. But I'd never dated anyone who I'd consider muscular or *buff*.

But being around Enzo on the lake... the sun glistening off of his skin, the way those shorts hugged his butt... man, I'd been in a state all day.

Yes, I was attracted to more than his body. Of course, I was. But seeing him today, and my reaction to him, I'd decided I was done being *good*. Done denying myself what I *really* wanted.

I was going to make a play, and *God help me*, Enzo was going to be right there with me.

He had to be.

We unloaded the trucks, said goodnight to the guys and walked back to his part of the compound.

My head was spinning, and my hands were shaking, as I formulated my plan. He must have been talking to me for a while, because when my name on his lips finally penetrated my brain, he was practically shouting and looking at me funny.

"Huh?" I asked.

"You're really lost in thought," he observed. "Everything okay?"

"Mm hm," I said noncommittally, putting my bag down next to the sofa and turning to him with a purpose. "What did you need?"

He stopped in front of me and searched my face. I'm not sure what he saw there but his voice lowered, and he said, "I just asked if you were hungry."

I reached out, grabbed his shirt, and stepped up to him.

"I am," I said throatily, brushing up close enough to touch him.

"*Melody,*" Enzo warned, his voice husky.

"*Lorenzo,*" I whispered back. "*You're fired.*"

Then I reached up and brought his face down to mine, my lips eagerly meeting his.

God, this has been a long time coming, I thought as the first touch ignited something within me.

Within us both.

I was jumping and he was lifting and then I was up in

his arms, his hands clutching my ass and my hands cradling his face.

The kiss was everything- sweet, sexy, and hot as hell.

He crossed the room, not stopping until my bottom hit the counter and he set me there. With the more secure position, our hands were free to roam, and we quickly divulged each other of our clothes, until we were left in only our bathing suits.

"Yes," I moaned when I got my hands on those abs and then spread them out to map out his body.

I felt the back of my top being untied and shifted so he could get it off, then leaned in and placed my mouth on his warm, sun-kissed skin. I felt his groan rumble against my lips and took it as encouragement to keep exploring.

I didn't get much terrain covered before I was distracted by his lips on my throat and then his tongue conducting its own exploration. I leaned back, giving him access to my breasts, and was not disappointed when he immediately gave them the attention they deserved.

Enzo sucked one hardened nipple into his mouth, while his hand explored the other breast. Everything felt so good, but when I realized I wasn't doing anything other than laying back and taking instead of giving, I sat up a little taller so that I could reach him with my hand.

My hand caressed his cock and he jumped back, breaths coming out in pants and his eyes as dark as midnight.

"The first time's gonna be quick," he said, almost apologetically.

I grinned at him and said, *"Thank God."* Because I

really didn't think I'd be able to handle drawn-out foreplay. I wanted him inside me.

He shucked off his trunks and I shifted to get my bottoms off, Enzo coming to help me once he was standing before me fully naked.

"You're beautiful," I told him, my eyes taking in their fill.

"You're gorgeous, Princess," Enzo said, reaching out to stroke my cheek as he looked me dead in the eyes. "Inside and out."

We reached for each other in tandem, and when he thrust inside of me, I saw a burst of light behind my eyelids. I started to lay back, but realized I was going to need to hold on, so I grasped his shoulders, wrapped my legs around his waist and did my best to participate.

Enzo shifted and angled himself just right, so that within a few thrusts I felt my orgasm building.

"Yes, Enzo, right there," I moaned, my head falling back as he sucked on my neck.

Pleasure shot through me, causing me to cry out, and Enzo moved faster, drawing it out until I was limp in his arms, his own following quickly behind.

Once we were both able to catch our breath, I lifted my head from where it had fallen on his shoulder and looked into his face. He was so handsome, it took my breath away, and I leaned in to kiss him soundly. This time enjoying the simplicity of the kiss rather than what it preluded.

When my world was spinning on its axis, Enzo shifted and dropped sweet kisses on my face before saying, "Now, let's take our time," and swept me up into his arms.

As he carried me up the stairs to his bed, I wondered how I was ever going to be able to leave him behind.

TWENTY-FIVE

ENZO

I *fucked up.*

It had been a late night. After I took Melody up to my bedroom, we'd made love two more times before finally falling asleep in each other's arms.

For all of my talk of professionalism and lines that shouldn't be crossed, all it had taken was two words from her to throw it all out the window... *you're fired.* She'd been so sexy and sure of herself in that moment, there was no way I would have been able to walk away. Not this time.

Did I regret? *Absolutely not.*

She was even better than my fantasies, and those had been really hot.

I woke to find her snuggled up against me, her skin soft and silky, her face sweet and innocent in her slumber.

I flashed back to what it had been like to have her in my bed. Under me. Over me. Curled up against my side. She'd been passionate, vocal, and free, and each second had been better than the last. It was the best night of my life, hands down, and I knew I was in deeper than even I'd realized.

It was more than infatuation. More than a crush on the gorgeous Nashville star. She was more than who the media portrayed her to be. More than the first impression she made on me. She was everything I'd been looking for in my life, in one perfect package.

I'd fallen for her, truly, madly, deeply, and it was more than I'd ever realized I could feel for someone.

It felt strange thinking and feeling this way, but as I looked down at the peaceful expression on her face, a little sigh escaped her lips, and my body flooded with tenderness. I lifted my hand to brush stray hair off her cheek and her eyes fluttered open.

Her lips curved into a sweet smile as she blinked up at me.

"Good morning," I said gruffly, struggling to keep the emotion out of my voice.

I was completely out of my depth here and unsure how to act.

"Good morning," she whispered back, her hand moving to caress my side, causing me to jump.

"Ticklish," I muttered as I struggled to keep still.

"Sorry," she said and moved to rub slow circles on my back instead.

"How'd you sleep?" I asked.

"Like a baby," Melody replied sleepily then her eyes popped open, and she sat up quickly causing the sheet to fall to her waist, leaving her beautiful breasts exposed.

God, her body is amazing.

"Oh my God, Dixie!" she exclaimed, jumping out of bed and running across the room and down the stairs completely naked.

I chuckled as I followed after her and yelled from the top of the stairs, "She's at Pop's remember? We'll go get her in a bit."

Melody came back around the corner and looked up at me.

"I forgot," she said with a sheepish grin. "I'm so used to having to let her out when I wake up that I freaked."

"It's understandable," I told her.

Damn, she looked amazing standing naked in my living room. I glanced automatically at the door to the hall leading to the rest of the compound and tried to remember if I locked it. The last thing I wanted was for one of the guys to walk in and see what I realized I wanted to be available for my eyes only.

I didn't want to share this view with anyone.

"How about I get dressed and then make us some breakfast," I suggested. "Then we can go pick up Dixie."

"I'd like that," Melody replied. "I'll start the coffee."

Obviously perfectly comfortable in her own skin, she moved to do just that, while I turned to at least throw some boxers on.

Since I was upstairs, I took the time to brush my teeth and slap on some deodorant as well, then went downstairs to the smell of coffee percolating. Assuming Melody had gone to freshen up as well, I pulled out some regular bacon, the plant-based bacon I'd found, eggs, and frozen hashbrowns.

Everything was cooking by the time Melody came out, showered and smelling amazing.

"Hey," she said softly, moving right to me and kissing me on my bare shoulder.

"Hey," I repeated back, grinning down at her. "Breakfast will be ready in a minute, but your coffee's ready."

We moved through the breakfast dance that we'd become accustomed to over the weeks, this time adding soft touches and sensual kisses to the routine.

As we were sitting down to eat, my phone rang, and I saw it was Smith.

"Hey, man," I said in greeting. "You're on speaker and Melody is here with me."

"Morning, Enzo; morning, Melody," Smith called out. "Sorry to call so early, but I wanted to let you know that we got another letter this morning. It wasn't signed, so although I'm sure it's another one from Chris Simon, I can't be positive. There haven't been any other emails or gifts, so I'm assuming he has a contact who will send his mail while he's in custody."

"What did it say?" I asked, keeping my eyes trained on Melody.

"More stuff about being her biggest fan, and about knowing the songs were written for me - the writer - but this time there was also something about making her pay for not sticking up for her biggest fans."

Melody's face turned ashen as he spoke.

"So, um, anyway, I was gonna call you next, Melody. Tomorrow is your testimony, so we'll need to do a call with the lawyer this evening to go over the dos and don'ts. Should I set it up for three or four o'clock?"

She cleared her throat and said, "Three works."

"I'll do that then, and I'll talk to you both later. Enzo, keep doing what you're doing, and keep Melody safe, okay?"

"Later, Smith," I said, then hung up and looked at Melody.

"Looks like you're rehired."

TWENTY-SIX

MELODY

I wasn't sure why I was so nervous. I wouldn't be in court, and it wasn't like I was about to go on the stand and be questioned and cross-examined.

It was more like a statement to the judge about what happened.

Still, I'd woken up early, unable to get my mind to settle down. And had spent the day basically pacing and wringing my hands as I waited for my appointed Zoom time with the judge. I'd taken time doing my hair and makeup and picked out an outfit that I felt made me look professional while giving me the confidence I would surely need.

Enzo offered to be in the room with me during the meeting, but I thought it would make me more nervous, so I told him I'd find him afterwards.

Now I was wishing he was there with me.

There was something about him that gave me strength, and I really could have used a little of it.

But at my request he'd left Tank and the guys

stationed outside and he'd gone off to spend some time with Gino and Mario. He hadn't wanted to leave me, but I'd insisted. Once Chris Simon was *hopefully* convicted, I'd be going back to Nashville and things would go back to normal for both of us.

After the night we'd shared, I'd kind of been hoping Enzo would ask me to stay. Or at least broach the subject of us trying to have a real relationship. I'd worked some things out in my mind, and I could see how living here and commuting to Nashville, when necessary, would work, especially if I could convince Enzo to let me build a studio. I may be getting ahead of myself, but I swear, the way he looked at me had me convinced he was feeling the same way... then Smith had called, and everything had kind of snowballed from there.

With another letter and the reminder of possible danger, Enzo had gone back to *head of security* mode and hadn't touched or kissed me since.

To be fair I hadn't gone to him last night either, choosing instead to lock myself in my room with Dixie and start a song about the way I'd felt finally being with Enzo. The buildup and anticipation had only made the night that much more explosive and fulfilling.

Enzo in the middle of the night whispering to me about his wants and feelings was going to stay with me forever.

That song was going to be my next number one hit. I could feel it.

I glanced at the clock and then moved to my laptop, which I'd placed at the table. After sitting down and taking a deep breath, I pressed the link my lawyer had sent me.

"Good afternoon, Ms. Miles," a professional-looking woman said to me when my video and microphone were connected. "Judge Preston will be with you shortly. Please know, this call will be recorded."

"Okay, thank you," I replied.

The judge came on and swore me in and then asked me to tell her what I knew about Chris Simon and detail the events of the night he came into my dressing room.

It was all over rather quickly, and when I disconnected after promising to be available, if necessary, I realized I'd freaked myself out for nothing. The judge had been even tempered and understanding, and although remembering that night wasn't fun, I was glad to have my statement on the record.

I closed my laptop and moved to the couch where I flopped down onto my back and was soon joined by Dixie, who jumped on my stomach.

I was emotionally exhausted.

"What's up, baby girl, you want to go outside?" I asked her.

She jumped down and trotted to the door, so I took that as a yes and went to slip on some sandals and grab her pink rhinestone-studded leash.

Rather than take her out back, I figured I'd better go through the front to let the guys know I was going to go on a quick walk. I was sure I'd be perfectly safe, but knew they had a job to do and didn't want to upset them by sneaking off.

"Hey, Tank, I'm just gonna go out with Dixie for a bit. I'll be right back," I said when I entered the open bay.

"I'll walk with you," he said, not so much asking as making a statement.

I didn't mind. The company would be nice.

"It's so nice out," I observed as we walked out into the sunshine.

"It is," Tank agreed as he fell into step beside me. "Did the call go okay?"

I nodded and said, "It did."

"That's good... must be a load off."

"Mm-hm."

"Something else bothering you?" he asked.

I glanced up at him and asked, "Why do you ask?"

He shrugged his massive shoulders and said, "Enzo's been a little... *testy,* the last twenty-four hours and you've seemed... *withdrawn.*" He spoke slowly like he was choosing his words carefully.

"I was just anxious about meeting with the judge," I said, then added, "And testy is one of Enzo's go-to moods, isn't it?"

I felt him watching me intently but kept walking and looking straight ahead.

I knew Enzo's rules for his business and was sure he didn't want me letting it slip that there was something between us that was anything other than professional. I mean, the vibe Tank was putting off said he probably already knew, but I wasn't about to confirm it for him.

We were quiet for a few moments, as we both watch Daisy sniff each blade of grass along the sidewalk, then finally she found the perfect place to do her business and we stopped walking.

"What do you think's gonna happen between you and Enzo once you're free to go back to Nashville?" Tank asked, and I swung my head up to look at him, surprised by his bluntness.

"Wow, you just went for it, huh?" I teased.

"Sometimes you gotta," he replied. "Look, Enzo's my guy. I've known him for a lotta years through a lotta shit, and I have never seen him as happy as he's been since I got here. And it looks to me like the biggest reason for that *is you*."

I cleared my throat and said, "Maybe it's being back in Mason Creek with his dad and brother that's made him happy."

Tank gave me a look that would have made me laugh if I didn't know how serious he was.

"Not buying it," he said. "How do *you* feel about *him*?"

My heart jumped into my throat at his questions because it's all I'd been asking myself since I woke up yesterday in his bed.

"Does it matter?" I asked softly.

"Of course it does."

"Like you said, I'll be heading back to Nashville soon. Plus, Enzo and I are *very* different people. I don't know how it would work between us," I admitted.

"Opposites make the best couples. Haven't you read, like, every book ever? If the two of you feel about each other the way *I think* you do, you'll make it work. What's the point of life? Work? Your zip code?" He shook his head emphatically. "No. It's finding a person who makes you happy, who you're excited to see, or just hear their voice on the phone. It's about sharing moments with the person you love most in the world."

"I didn't realize you were such a romantic," I said, his words hitting their mark.

"Romance is the best part of life. All I'm saying is you should think about it... think about Enzo and search inside yourself to see how he makes you feel, and then picture your life without him."

I nodded and we turned around to head back home.

What I didn't say, was that I'd already considered what my life would look like when I got back to Nashville, and there was an Enzo-sized hole in it. And, funnily enough, I'd also have holes where Mario, Tank, and even Gino and Tate were. I didn't have a lot of time for friends or a social life in Nashville, and I'd forgotten how wonderful it was to spend time with people who had no ulterior motives.

To actually live a full life.

TWENTY-SEVEN

ENZO

"It turns out it was his second offense, so because Simon came into her dressing room, made her feel threatened and like he may be violent toward her, and because of the nature of some of the correspondence and gifts he sent, the judge sentenced him to one year in prison. And he's been ordered to cease all contact with her from now on."

"That's great, so you're comfortable with her coming back to Nashville and resuming her life?" I asked, a pit of despair settling in my stomach.

Of course, I was happy for Melody, but I hated the thought of her leaving.

"Yeah, and I figured she'd rather hear it from you in person, rather than over the phone from me or the lawyer," Smith said.

"Okay, I'll let her know. I'm sure she'll be relieved."

"Tell her I'll call later to go over her travel arrangements," he said, and I never wished I could punch someone over the phone so badly.

"Will do."

I hung up and walked into my dad's living room, where she, Pops, and Gino were watching Dixie and Rocky play with each other. They were laughing merrily as the kitten ran after the dog.

Rocky was actually bigger than Dixie now.

"Hey, who was on the phone?" my dad asked when he noticed me lingering by the door.

"It was Smith," I answered, my eyes on Melody.

Her eyes caught mine as she asked, "And?"

"And... it's over. He's been sentenced to one year and it's safe for you to go home."

She got to her feet with a *whoop* and ran to me. I braced myself, so when she flew into my arms, I was ready to catch her.

"That's wonderful," she said with a choked laugh. "I can't believe it's over."

I held her close, inhaling the sweet scent of her and memorizing the way she felt against me.

"So, what does that mean?" Pops asked. "Will you be leaving?"

Melody turned but kept one arm wrapped around my waist.

"Yes. I have a new album to write and shows to play in Nashville. It's time to get back to work."

"Smith said he'll call you later to get everything scheduled," I told her numbly.

"But you'll come back, right?" Gino asked. "It's not like the road to Nashville is a one-way street."

"Of course, I'd love to come back and see you all," she

said, and I swear it felt like every eye in the room was boring into my skull.

"Well, we better get going," I said suddenly, unable to stand the scrutiny. "Gino, I'll see you bright and early tomorrow for your first day."

Melody didn't say anything, but simply watched me closely as she said her goodbyes and gathered Dixie's things.

The cab of my truck on the ride back to the compound was silent and there was this overwhelming feeling of melancholy. I noticed Melody staring out the window as we drove through town, her eyes watching the kids throwing frisbees and flying kites on the square, their faces sticky from ice cream.

"It's such a lovely town," she murmured, and then I swore she said, "A wonderful place to raise a family."

I glanced over at her, but she kept her eyes trained out the window.

When we got home, we bypassed the main entrance for my private entrance around back, neither of us wanting to make small talk with the guys. Not in the headspace we both seemed to be living in.

Once we were inside and Melody filled Dixie's bowls, she moved to where I was standing in the center of the room, feeling *and I'm sure looking* lost, and put her arms around my waist.

I felt her hands reach around and grab my ass, and a surprised laugh came out of me.

I shifted to look down at her and found her eyes on my lips. Not needing any further invitation, I kissed her soundly, taking my time exploring and committing every taste to memory.

Once we were both worked up, I broke away and asked with a smirk, "Guess I'm fired again?"

Melody grinned and said, "So fired."

I lifted her smoothly and laid her down on the couch, my hands grasping her ankles and moving up over her calves and then her thighs, taking the skirt of her dress with them, not stopping until I reached the scrap of lace at her center.

Her eyes tracked my movements, darkening with each brush of my fingertips against her heated skin.

I brushed my thumbs over her panties, and she writhed beneath me, her hips lifting, indicating she wanted me to keep going. I maneuvered her until she was in the perfect position, and then knelt before her like she was my altar and I was ready to worship.

Melody moved her arms above her head and grasped onto the back of the sofa as my lips met her inner thigh. When she gasped, I bit her lightly, then caressed the reddened skin with my tongue.

When her skin was peppered with love bites, I shot her a wicked grin and moved my hands beneath her ass to remove the lace, then held on tight as I shifted her hips upward, and dove in.

She bucked beneath me, crying out words of encouragement and sometimes directions, until coming beneath my mouth with the sweet sound of my name on her lips.

TWENTY-EIGHT

MELODY

The day had been perfect...

I'd woken up feeling satisfied and glorious. We'd spent another night making love, my stalker was officially behind bars, and Enzo had been sweet and attentive all day.

We'd spent all morning in town square, shopping, having pizza for lunch at Sauce It Up, and walking hand in hand as we got to know each other better. Enzo had been first to take my hand when we'd started our walking tour with window shopping.

I'd been pleasantly surprised, and he'd kept surprising me throughout our wanderings.

He'd bought me some sexy lingerie at Queen's Unmentionables, and we'd found the perfect book to give Tank at One More Chapter, and although he'd protested, I did end up buying him a watch at King's Jewelry.

Now, we were picking out ice cream at Twisted Sisters Ice Cream Shack and were going to sit out on the blanket Enzo pulled out of the back of his truck and have a little makeshift picnic in the park.

"Can I get two scoops of the huckleberry?" Enzo asked, then looked at me to go next.

I'd been looking at the menu for five minutes and couldn't make up my mind. Finally, I said, "I'll try the cherry twist."

"It's nice to see the auction worked out for you," one of the sisters who ran the shack, Hattie, said to us with a smile.

Enzo chuckled and thanked her for the ice cream but didn't respond to her statement.

Since his hands were full, I tucked my free hand in the crook of his arm as we set off to find the perfect spot.

He led me out of the town square and across the street to where there was a picnic area by the creek. It was beautiful, with the spring flowers blooming happily in the summer sun, and the sound of the water running over rocks in the creek.

Enzo laid out the blanket on the bank and we both sat down, stretching our legs out in front of us as we worked on eating our ice cream before it melted.

"You must have loved growing up here," I mused as I took in the peaceful ambiance.

It was so much different than the concrete jungle I'd grown up in.

"I really did," Enzo said, leaning back to rest on his elbows. "We rode our bikes everywhere, spent as much time outside as possible, and had to be really sneaky when it came to doing things our parents didn't want. In a town this small, it's nearly impossible to get away with anything. Someone always seems to notice, and it always sent through the grapevine. So, we took it as a sort of challenge... Who could drink beer in the woods, hold a bonfire, or make out at the old man Davis's bridge, without it getting back to their parents?" He laughed and shook his head as if reliving a memory. "My buddy Mitch was actually pretty good at not getting caught, but Gino? Man, he didn't get away with anything. It was almost like Pops had a GPS tracker on him or something."

"It's a good thing they didn't have GPS, or social media, back then. Can you imagine the amount of trouble it would have caused? I almost feel bad for kids these days."

Enzo glanced at me and said, "Must be terrible. I wouldn't want anyone to have been videotaping the dumb shit I did as a teenager."

"Same," I agreed.

"Like what?" he asked.

"Okay, well, we didn't do much bike riding or anything like that, but we would sneak out and take the subway to Broadway or to the clubs we knew didn't check ID. My parents would have killed me if they knew any of it. In fact, I've still never told them. I don't know if I ever will. What they don't know won't hurt them, right?"

"Pops knows everything," Enzo said, his lips quirking up. "Most of it he thought was funny, but he did get mad when I told him that usually when I told him I was staying over at Mitch's house, I was really with a girl sleeping out in an old barn on her family's property."

"I bet you were a rascal," I teased, finishing up my ice

cream and laying back on the blanket as I looked up at his profile.

He glanced down at me and snorted. "A rascal?"

"Did you just snort?"

"Did you just call me *a rascal*?" he asked again. "What is this, the forties?"

I nudged his leg with the toe of my sandal and said, "You know what I mean…"

"I do, but I think you'd actually be surprised. I'm not as much of a lothario as you seem to think. I was with a couple girls in high school and a few over the years when I was in the military, but never anyone serious."

"You've never had a girlfriend?" I asked, and I was surprised. I would have thought women would have been fighting for the title. "I know you said before that you've never been really serious about anyone, but I figured you'd still dated and had girlfriends."

"Nope."

"Huh," I said, turning my head to look up at the clouds in the sky. "I've had a couple boyfriends, but we never got to the point where a proposal was eminent. I think I was always too career driven and that kind of scared them off, or they thought I wasn't focused enough on them, you know?"

"Some guys can't handle a strong, independent woman," Enzo said, laying back to join me.

We turned our heads, so we were gazing into each other's eyes.

"They're not secure enough in their manhood to allow the woman to be the breadwinner in the relationship. To understand that her goals and aspirations are just as important as his. To let go of the gender roles they were raised with."

I reached out to trace his face with the tip of my finger.

"I love the way your mind works," I told him softly. "And how tender your heart is... How you're this big tough guy on the outside, but there's so much more to you than the image you portray."

"Right back at you, babe."

I shifted closer and brushed my lips against his, only to be pulled on top of him. What I'd meant to be a quick kiss turned into a full-on make-out session. When I realized we were rolling around in a public park, I sat up with a giggle.

"Maybe we should head back home," I suggested.

"Probably a good idea," Enzo said with a sexy grin.

We got up and as he bent to pick up and fold the blanket, I noticed something on the picnic table a few feet away.

"What's that?" I wondered aloud and moved to get a closer look.

When I got close enough, I saw that it was a stuffed animal with a note attached that had *Melody* written on the outside. That's when I screamed.

TWENTY-NINE

ENZO

I dropped the blanket and ran toward her as soon as I heard her scream. No longer thinking of all the things I'd do to her when we got home, protector mode kicked right in, as a chill ran down my spine at the sound of Melody in distress.

"What is it?" I asked, adding, "Back away," as I joined her.

I leaned in and listened, to see if the bear was emitting any sound, as my eyes surveyed the park for any other sign of life.

I didn't hear anything, so I picked it up and ripped the head off, just to be sure there was nothing inside.

It was empty, so I unpinned the note and read it.

It's all your fault.

I swung around, still looking but not seeing anyone else on this side of the street. And those I saw across the street, I knew.

"Did you notice anyone?" I asked her when I was satisfied whoever had left the gift was no longer there.

Melody shook her head, her eyes wide and filling with tears.

Fuck, I thought as I crossed to her and tucked her into my side. "Let's go," I said and urged her to start walking.

I knew this would happen. I let my guard down and crossed lines I knew I shouldn't cross, and someone walked right up beside us without me realizing it. I was so caught up in Melody that I put her at risk.

We hurried to my truck and got in, and as I drove through town toward the sheriff's station, I kept my eyes peeled for anyone or anything that looked out of place.

I called Tank on the drive to let him know what happened and that we'd be on our way after I spoke with the sheriff and to brief the guys.

We got out of the truck and walked inside.

"Sit there," I told Melody, pointing to the bench across from the front desk. "The sheriff doesn't allow civilians into the back but no one's out front, so I'm going to get someone and let them know what's going on and then we'll head to the compound."

Melody nodded and wrapped her arms around herself.

I strode into the back and went up to Sam, one of the deputies and the only person I saw in the room.

"Hey, Sam, is the sheriff around, or Aiden?" I asked, looking toward their empty offices.

"No, Enzo, they're out on a call. Is there something I can help you with?" he asked.

"You know about my client, Melody Miles." He nodded. "There was just an incident over by the picnic area at the creek. Someone left her a stuffed animal with a note that said, *'It's all your fault'*. Once we saw it, whoever put it there was gone, so I just wanted to let the sheriff know so you guys could be on the lookout for anyone strange or suspicious, and also that my guys will be out looking around town for the same."

"Okay, Enzo, I'll let them know. Don't worry, we'll find whoever's messing with Ms. Miles."

I walked back out to the front and saw the bench was empty.

I whirled to Bess, the dispatcher who was currently standing at the desk dropping off a pile of folders.

"Where is she?" I asked, assuming she'd gone to the restroom.

"Where's who, honey?" Bess asked.

"*Melody!*" I shouted. "Melody Miles."

"I haven't seen her," she replied, looking worriedly at Sam as he came running at my shout.

"She was sitting right there," I said, pointing desperately at the bench as my stomach tightened and my heart began to pound.

"We'll find her," Sam said. "Bess, check the Ladies."

I ran out the door and looked up and down the street, then across the square, my eyes landing on the ice cream stand we'd gone to earlier, before swiveling to search the square.

Nothing.

I took my phone out of my pocket and called Tank. "Get down to the square now. Melody's missing." And hung up.

"She's not inside," Sam said as he joined me on the sidewalk.

"My guys are on their way, but for now, I'll go left, you go right, yeah? She couldn't have gotten far."

I didn't wait for him to answer but took off past the bank and across the street, holding my hand up to stop an oncoming car from hitting me. Noticing the beauty salon, with its big bay window overlooking the street, I ran to the door and went inside.

All eyes turned to me, and I knew I must look frantic when Faith stopped cutting the woman in front of hers' hair and asked, "Enzo, are you okay?"

"Has anyone seen Melody in the last few minutes?"

"That pretty country singer?" A stylist I didn't know asked.

I nodded.

"Sure, yeah, I saw her walking by just a bit ago. Looked like she was limping."

"Was she alone?" I asked, my heart leaping at the lead.

She shook her head and said, "No, hon, she was with a heavyset woman with dark hair and glasses."

"A woman? You're sure?" I asked. "Do you happen to remember which way they were going?"

"Yeah, right down that way," she said, pointing the brush she was holding. "Toward Wren's. And, yes, I'm sure it was a woman. The way she was dressed showed off her assets if you know what I mean."

"I'm sorry we didn't stop them, Enzo," Faith said, worried. "I guess we just thought the stalker was a man, not a woman."

"Yeah, me too. Thank you," I said, and I swear, if I

had the time, I would have kissed that hairdresser. Instead, I turned and exited as quickly as I'd entered.

I pulled out my phone as I darted down the street.

"She was seen with a heavyset woman with dark hair, glasses, and exposed cleavage," I told Tank when he answered. "Last seen headed toward Wren's on foot."

"Got it."

"Have everyone spread out," I told him. "And Tank... Just... find her."

"We will, boss."

THIRTY

MELODY

"You don't have to do this," I said, mimicking every cop show or movie I'd ever seen.

"*Shut up*," my captor said aggressively for the third time since she'd walked into the sheriff's station and pointed a gun at me.

"Get up and walk out the door without so much as a peep. If you don't, I will shoot you in the gut and your sexy man in the back of the head," she'd whispered in my ear.

I'd been so freaked out and intent on keeping Enzo in my field of vision, that I hadn't heard the door open. I'd turned to look at her and found a stranger with a menacing expression staring back at me.

When I looked back to see if Enzo was looking back at me... *please, God, let him be looking...* I could no longer see him.

Because she sounded like she was telling the truth, I stood up and moved to the door. Once we were outside, she jammed the gun in my side and walked a half step behind me so people walking by wouldn't be able to see it.

As we passed the shops, I tried to look inside in hopes someone would be standing close enough to the window to meet my eyes, but either they weren't, or they didn't look up before we passed.

I tried talking to her, to show her I was a person, like they say to do on those same shows, but so far, she hadn't said anything more to me other than *shut up*.

"He's going to see I'm gone and come looking for me," I told her as we turned off of the main street and started down an alley. "If you would just tell me what you want..."

"I want my husband back, can you make that happen?" she seethed, pushing the barrel of the gun harder into my side.

"Who is your husband?" I asked.

I wasn't expecting her to shove me, and I went down onto the gravel on my bare knees. I bit back a cry at the sting, not wanting to make her angrier than she already was.

"My God, you are an *idiot*. I have no idea what he saw in you."

I closed my eyes, expecting some sort of blow, or, God forbid, a gunshot Instead I felt her fingers dig into my bicep as she tried to lift me back onto my feet.

"*Get up, Princess*," she said, and I *hated* that she called me that.

Once I was on my feet, she resumed her previous position and gave me a shove to get my feet moving.

When we reached the woods I paused, not wanting

to lose visibility, but she put a hand on my shoulder and squeezed it saying, "Move your ass," so I kept moving.

"Is Chris Simon your husband?" I asked once we were deeper into the woods.

Even though I hadn't known he was married, it was the only answer that made any sense.

"Ding, ding, ding, give the girl a prize," she said sarcastically. "I knew you'd ruin our lives the first time Chris saw one of your music videos. The way he watched you on that screen... he'd never looked at me like that before. *Never*. And after that it just got worse. He became obsessed. Buying all your CD's and merch. Going to all your shows, watching all your specials. He wouldn't do anything unless it involved you in some way. He was your number one fan, and how did you repay him? Repay that love and devotion? You put him in freaking *prison*! Now I'm left alone with a mountain of bills and no husband at home. He doesn't even let me visit him."

"I'm sorry," I stammered. "Truly. I never wanted to cause anyone harm or pain."

"Well, you did, and now you've got to pay."

She pushed me again, and as much as I tried to look around for any sort of landmark that would help me find my way out of here, everything looked the same.

"Mrs. Simon," I said, hoping it would help to use her name. "I'm sorry that you're hurting. What can I do to help?"

"Really, the only way I see Chris moving on, is if you're no longer around as an option."

Jesus, she's even crazier than he is.

"You're gonna have to die."

By the time we reached a section of the creek I'd never been to, with a bridge that I would have described as magical under different circumstances, I was absolutely terrified. In fact, my legs were shaking so bad I could barely walk another step.

"Get on the bridge," she ordered, her voice low and mean.

I walked up until I was on the center of the bridge and turned around to look at her, hopeful that having her look me in the face would make things more difficult for her.

"Mrs. Simon," I started again. "I'm sorry about what's happened to you, but you have to know that doing this won't make things better. It will only make them much, much worse."

"It's the only thing that will make him see *I'm* the one who loves him and will be there for him when he gets out. You're the monster who put him there. How can he love you?"

I wasn't sure how to play this. I didn't think telling her she was wrong would help, or talking about his obsession with me, but I knew I had to do something. I couldn't just stand there defenseless and let this happen.

"Don't you deserve someone who loves you as much as you obviously love him?"

"I do... I've done everything to make him see me. I've dyed my hair, bought new clothes. But nothing worked. He only has eyes for you. You have to understand, even when he gets out, he's not going to move on. He'll go back to doing the same things he did before he went to jail."

Those words scared me almost as much as the gun she was holding.

"He's been ordered not to contact me again. Not now. Not ever," I told her.

"You think that matters?" she cried. "He won't be able to stop, no matter what some judge says. He's going to keep at it until he gets what he wants. *You.* Unless *I* take you out of the equation."

THIRTY-ONE

ENZO

As I got to Wren's I saw Ashley walking inside.

"Ashley, did you see Melody?" I asked.

"Yeah, with some-"

"Which way did they go?" I asked quickly not needing to hear the rest.

"Past Java Jitters."

"Thanks!" I yelled as I took off running in that direction.

My phone rang and I hit accept when I saw Tank's name.

"Talk to me."

"A man just told us they saw them walking across the street by the bookstore. And that the taller woman took them as far away from the fire station as possible but kept looking back at it until they disappeared into the trees."

"So, the woods," I stated, changing my direction and sprinting as I pressed disconnect.

By the time I got to the edge of the woods near the

fire station, all of my guys, Sam, Aiden and Gino were jogging over.

"The only things back there are the back of the apartments, the entrance to Baylor Lake and old man Davis's bridge. Let's split up and find her. They couldn't have gotten far. Assume this woman is armed and dangerous," I told them, and we all broke off and started into the woods.

Gino met up with me and asked, "To the bridge?"

I nodded and we headed in that direction, eyes, and ears open as we hoped for something to indicate we were going in the right direction.

When we broke through the clearing that led to the bridge, I heard the faint sound of voices and motioned to Gino. He nodded, indicating he'd heard it too. I stopped long enough to reach for the gun I kept strapped to my ankle, then started toward them, hopeful over the fact I heard two voices, one of them Melody's.

"He's been ordered not to contact me again. Not now. Not ever," I heard Melody say.

Gino and I split up, so we'd come up on either side of them, and crouched low to the ground as we did our best to move soundlessly.

"You think that matters?" the other woman cried. "He won't be able to stop, no matter what some judge says. He's going to keep at it until he gets what he wants. *You.* Unless *I* take you out of the equation."

My blood ran cold at her words, and nearly froze when I saw the gun she had pointed at Melody.

I rushed over, stood tall, and lifted my gun.

"Put the weapon down and step away," I ordered, my voice loud and sharp.

The woman turned toward the sound of my voice and lowered her arms slightly, which was enough for Gino to come at her in a flying tackle.

The gun went off, and my world stopped momentarily as I worried either Gino or Melody were hit. But instinct kicked in and I rushed over to kick the weapon farther out of her reach as Gino pushed her over onto her stomach and held her hands behind her back.

"Call Sam or Aiden," he said, but I already had my phone in my hand.

"I'm here," Sam called as he hurried to join us and take over securing the woman.

I looked up to see Melody still standing on the bridge.

"Melody," I called, and the sound of my voice seemed to put her in motion. She ran off the bridge, keeping a wide birth from her captor, and flew into my arms.

Relieved everyone was unharmed, I let out a deep breath and hugged her tight.

Alerted by the gunshot, everyone joined us and came to tell Melody they were glad she was okay and promised to buy Gino a drink for the tackle. The story was getting more outlandish with each retelling.

Once Melody had given a statement to the deputy and promised to be available if they had any further questions, we left Mrs. Simon in the custody of the sheriff's department and headed back to the station to get my truck and go home.

When we pulled up in front of my house, Pops was pacing outside while Dixie ran around him in circles. He must have heard the truck approach because he looked up, his eyes went straight to the passenger side, and his face cleared.

I think he even did the sign of the cross before hurrying to meet us and opened Melody's door.

"*Thank God*," he murmured, and once she stepped down, he gathered her into his arms. "Gino called me, and I came right over. Let's get you inside. Some tea and maybe some of those lemon cookies you like will help."

I watched him take her inside, Dixie trailing after them, as the guys pulled up and joined me.

"When did Pops become Ma?" I asked Gino, in an attempt to lighten the moment.

"He's always been like that when one of us was sick or injured."

Yeah, I thought, *but never with anyone but us or Tate.*

"I can't thank you all enough for responding so quickly. She's safe because we were all there."

"Not just us," Tank said. "The whole town helped. If they hadn't made some of the observations they did, we may not have gotten there in time. Looks like you'll have to go to Pony Up this weekend and buy a round for everybody. They deserve it."

I nodded, realizing what he said was true.

I'd known I could count on the people of Mason Creek to keep Melody's presence here a secret, I hadn't realized I could also count on them to help keep her safe.

THIRTY-TWO

MELODY

To say I'd been shaken was an understatement. But Mario had been so sweet and attentive that I hadn't had the heart to tell him that all I really wanted to do was crawl into bed.

Enzo, however, must have read it on my face, because after allowing Mario to fuss for a bit, Enzo sent him and Gino home and promised to call if we needed anything. Then he'd suggested I go get washed up and get some rest.

I'd been so grateful that he'd understood what I needed, but when hours passed and the only one in my bed offering me comfort was Dixie, I couldn't deny that I was disappointed and a little heartbroken.

The next day had been spent making plans with Smith to get me home and back to the grind.

Both the Simons were off the streets, and I was once again safe and free to live my life.

I wouldn't deny the fact that as I packed, I hoped Enzo would sweep into my room and beg me to stay. But

I'd felt the shift between us and knew he was distancing himself. He was upset that he'd let his guard down and Simon's wife had come to his town and gotten to me right under his nose.

And of course, I understood where he was coming from. But I'd hoped his feelings for me would outweigh his regret.

Maybe this was how he coped and guarded his heart. He had admitted repeatedly that he'd never had a serious relationship or girlfriend, so although in my mind I was the perfect candidate to be the first, maybe Enzo didn't have it in him.

It may be silly, but I wanted *him* to come to *me*. I didn't want to *beg* him to love me and want me in his life. I'd already made the first move *twice*. It was his turn.

I double checked I had everything, of mine and Dixie's, then took my carry-on bag outside to join the rest of my bags, which were already being loaded into Enzo's truck. All the guys were there, except Ty and Snape, who were on assignment, along with Gino and Mario.

Tank and Enzo loaded everything up while I said my goodbyes.

"You better come back and visit soon," Mario said with a frown.

"I will, and you can come see me in Nashville, too. Anytime," I told him, giving him a big hug.

"When you come back, I'll take you to the gym," Gino said. I'd told him I'd hated how helpless I felt on that bridge and that I wish I knew how to defend myself. He promised to teach me.

"I'll hold you to it."

"Here, take this," Tank said, handing me a copy of *Small Town Girl* by LaVyrle Spencer. "For the plane."

"What's it about?" I asked him, taking it and turning it over.

"Read it and see," he replied, then lowered his head to give me a kiss on the cheek. "Don't be a stranger."

I nodded, touched, and turned to get in the truck before I did something embarrassing, like crying like a baby.

The drive back to the airport was long and quiet.

I had Dixie snoozing on my lap and Tank's book clutched in my hand. I watched out the window as we got farther and farther away from Mason Creek and felt like I was leaving a little bit of myself behind.

When we got to the airport, Enzo loaded my things onto a cart while I secured Dixie in her stroller, and then called someone over to help me get to first class check in.

"Well, I guess this is it," he said, and I wanted to shake him.

I wanted to say, *Fight for me. For us. Don't let what could be the best thing to happen to either of us go. Tell me you love me. Ask me how we can make it work.*

But I didn't. And neither did he.

"Yeah, uh, thanks for everything," I said lamely, feeling like my heart was shattering.

"Anytime," Enzo said, his eyes darting to the stroller and back to me. "Have a safe trip and let us know when you make it home safely."

Us. Not me.

"I will," I promised.

He gave me an awkward hug and moved around the

truck and got in it, while I told the man with my bags I was ready to go.

I made it to my flight without crying. I'd save that for when I was in my own bed. When Dixie and I settled into my seat and the flight attendant asked if I'd like a glass of champagne, I was actually tempted.

The thought of numbing myself with alcohol for once sounded appealing, which was why I knew I didn't need it.

"I'll have a ginger ale, please."

"Yes, ma'am," he said, and moved to get it from the galley.

I took a notebook and pen out of my bag and started to write. By the time I landed in Nashville I had drafts about life-changing love, small-town romance, how to handle heartbreak, and my favorite, how clueless men could be.

When we got down to the baggage claim in Nashville Smith was waiting.

"Oh, thank God," he said, giving me a hug and a tearful smile. "I can't believe what Simon's wife did. I'm so grateful you're okay and this is all finally over."

"Me, too," I agreed. "I'm eager to sleep in my own bed and get into the studio."

"I've got you booked for tomorrow as requested. And I had the cleaners go through your house yesterday and your chef stocked your fridge, so everything is set for you at home."

"I appreciate it, Smith," I thought, thinking how strange it was going to feel to eat alone again.

I pushed the thought away - *I need to get home before*

I break down - determined to focus on the things I was grateful for, rather than what I was missing.

As we walked out of the airport, just before I reached the waiting car, a paparazzo stepped out in front of me and said, "Melody, over here. It's so good to have you back in Nashville. Did you have a nice vacation?"

I posed for a few shots, knowing if I didn't, they would take one anyway and post it no matter how terrible it was, and said, "Yes, I did. But it's great to be back in *Music City*!"

THIRTY-THREE

ENZO

"To the citizens of Mason Creek!" Gino yelled. He was standing on the stage at *Pony Up* in between acts. We'd just come through on our promise to buy everyone a drink after they helped us save Melody and capture her abductor. "You are all brave, fierce warriors, and we are so grateful you helped us rescue the fair maiden, Melody Miles."

A chorus of cheers filled the bar. It was late in the night, so most everyone had already had a few. Add in Gino's penchant for drama and the place was feeling downright jovial.

I shook my head at my brother's speech and looked down at my beer.

"Come on, man," Tank said, clapping a large hand on my back. "You've been a grump ever since Melody got on that plane. Why don't you just suck it up, admit you miss her, and give her a call?"

I snorted. *As if I hadn't thought about doing just that every second of every day.*

"You saw her on TV," I muttered, then mimicked, *"It's great to be back in Music City.* She's happy and back where she belongs doing what she loves."

"You know that's just media stuff, Enzo," Tank argued. "You've been around enough celebrities to know how they have to spin things. That's Melody *the superstar*, but you know the real Melody, and you know as well as I do that she was happy *here. With you.*"

"I know no such thing," I said, then furrowed my brow. "Does that even make sense?" I tried again, "I don't know any such thing."

"You're being an idiot," he said, and walked away.

Good. I wanted to be alone with my beer anyway.

"Hey there, brother," Gino said, taking the seat Tank had just vacated.

I groaned. "What?"

"Jeez, what a sweet greeting," Gino said sarcastically. "You still got a bug up your ass over Melody leaving?"

I glared at him.

"She called us, you know. Me and Pop."

I scowled and downed my beer. "So?"

"So, she's doing good. In the studio, working on music. She sounded much better."

"*Great.*"

"Why don't I think you mean that?" he asked, looking closely at me.

"I don't know, Gino? Why do you believe in paranormal activity and aliens? Because you live with your head in the clouds. Why are you telling me this?"

"Wow, shots fired," Gino said, surprised at my outburst.

"What's going on over here?" our dad asked, taking the empty seat on the other side of me.

"Enzo's feeling sorry for himself and drowning his sorrows," my brother said.

"*Fuck you*," was my reply.

"Hey, easy. What's got you in such a mood? We're celebrating here," Pops asked.

"I need another beer," I said, starting to stand when my dad stopped me by putting his hand on my arm and saying, "S*it*."

"Now tell me what this is about."

I wanted to hold onto my anger. To tell everyone to go to hell and storm out of the bar, but something about my dad's voice had the anger receding and the sorrow seeping in.

"She's gone," I said miserably.

"Of course she's gone. You drove her to the airport," Pops said, and I felt some of the anger creeping back.

"Did you even tell her you wanted her to stay?" Gino asked. "Or that you wanted to be with her? That you *love* her?"

I sighed and let my shoulders hunch. "No."

"Then what did you expect, son? She's not a mind reader."

"I know that," I argued.

"Do you?" he asked. "Because you let her go and then proceeded to mope around like a grumpy bear."

"Look, we're complete opposites, okay? What good would staying in Mason Creek do her? She's got a life and a career in Nashville."

"I'd say she also has the kind of job, and money, that she could work from anywhere. So... next?" Gino said.

"What?"

"What's your next excuse?"

"I'm seriously about to punch you," I told him, but he only grinned at me.

"I am not breaking up a bar fight," Pops said wryly.

Pops had broken up plenty of our fights when we were younger, but now I was all talk. I'd never actually fight my brother. Not even when he was being a know-it-all asshole.

"I let my defenses down, forgot about my rules, and crossed the line with Melody. And doing so put her in danger. I was supposed to protect her, and I failed."

"There it is," Gino said, which made me have second thoughts about not fighting him. "You're being some kind of martyr because you think you let her down. But you didn't. You're human. The tough, strong, Marine, *Lorenzo Fratelli*, is human, just like the rest of us. You're not infallible, and you're not to blame for the actions of a woman who was unhinged."

"He's right, son. Loving someone isn't a weakness," Pops said. "I've never seen you with anyone the way you were with Melody. She's your perfect match. The other piece to your puzzle."

"What if she doesn't feel the same way about me that I do about her?" That was my real fear. What if I put myself out there, laid my heart on the line, and she didn't reciprocate my feelings?

"Enzo, the only people who don't seem to know that you and Melody are crazy in love with each other, are you and Melody," Gino said with a laugh. "It's, like, totally obvious. You're so in love it makes me nauseous to see."

I grinned at him and asked, "Really, you think so?"

Gino stood up and realizing what he was about to do I put up my hand and said, "Don't," but it was too late.

He rushed to the stage, grabbed the mic off the stand and asked, "Who here thinks Enzo and Melody belong together?"

The entire bar started cheering.

THIRTY-FOUR

MELODY

"That was a great one," Mike, one of the guys I worked with in my recording studio said. "Want to go again?"

"Yeah, I'd like to try something different at the end," I told him.

I'd been at it for hours but was so close to getting it exactly how I wanted, I couldn't stop yet.

This often happened when I was in the studio. I'd work tirelessly, hours on end, often well into the night. There was something so exciting and energizing to me about recording a song or a whole album.

Behind performing live, it was my favorite part of the job.

But since I was doing an impromptu acoustic show that night, once we finished that final take, I had to thank everyone and take off.

Dixie was at home, but I had a dog walker who came and played with her and took her out when I was working and she couldn't come along, so I knew she was fine.

Since she was taken care of, I told my driver to take me straight to the venue on Lower Broadway.

It was late and there were people everywhere, so I had my driver take me around to the back entrance where I was able to slip in without being noticed.

I could hear someone already on stage and made my way through the familiar hallway to the dressing room in back.

"Good evening, Ms. Miles," one of the managers called as I reached the door. "The room is ready for you and your assistant dropped off the clothes you requested. Can I have a meal prepared or get you anything?"

At the mention of food, my stomach growled, and I realized I hadn't eaten all day.

"I would love some of your whole wheat truffle macaroni," I told him. "And some water."

"The water is already inside. I'll get that mac and cheese going for you, just holler if you need anything else."

"I will, thanks."

I let myself in and put my things down before pouring water into the glass, which was filled with ice, then I sat down and let out a sigh. It was the first moment I'd had to think all day, so of course, thoughts of Enzo started creeping in.

This was why I'd kept myself busy since I'd arrived back in Nashville. I wanted to pour my emotions into the music, not sit down and feel them.

I pulled out my phone and opened the few pictures I'd taken of Enzo, and just as I had all week, wished I'd taken more. There was one of him driving the boat at the lake, him and Tank talking in the compound, Enzo asleep on the couch with Dixie in his lap, and finally, one of us laying on the picnic blanket outside right before I'd seen the stuffed bear, and everything had gone crazy.

I felt tears prick the corners of my eyes and put the phone away.

I'd wait until after I ate to get dressed, but I could start retouching my makeup just to give myself some sort of distraction.

The manager brought me the food himself, then left me to eat it in private before coming back to tell me they were ready for me onstage.

I'd dressed in cowboy boots, a pretty floral dress, and a denim vest, with my favorite cowboy hat completing the look. My stomach was full of nerves, but that was normal, and I thrived on the nervous energy that accompanied a performance.

It meant the music was still important to me and I cared about pleasing my fans.

"We have a special treat for ya'll tonight," the announcer was saying. "Please welcome to the stage... *Melody Miles*."

I heard a few gasps and then cheers and clapping.

I did these surprise shows every once in a while, usually in between the big tours. It was always fun to see the looks on the audience's faces when I stepped out and they saw it really was me.

"Thank you," I told the announcer, then looked out into the crowd as I got myself situated.

There was a stool already set up, with a standing mic, and my guitar in its stand next to it.

"How's everyone doing tonight?" I asked once I was seated and had my guitar resting across my lap. "I hope you don't mind me crashing your party," I added with a laugh as they screamed. "I thought it would be fun to strip it down for you tonight and play a couple new songs I've been working on. What do you think? Is that okay?"

The bar erupted in cheers once more and I smiled out at everyone before lifting my guitar and playing the first note.

The room went silent as I began to sing.

I started with song Tucker and I had written together in Mason Creek before transitioning into the songs about love and heartbreak.

The crowd was with me the whole way. Sometimes swaying to the music, sometimes slow dancing, and others simply sitting down and enjoying the show. By the time I got to the last, and most emotional song, I was caught up in the sentiment and my voice was starting to crack with it.

When I got to the part where I asked why he didn't beg me to stay, I glanced up and saw Enzo standing in front of the stage.

I blinked thinking it was all in my head, but he was still there, and I was hit with three emotions at once... *elation, anger, and hope.*

THIRTY-FIVE

ENZO

I got the hint.
From the whole town.
I'd woken up the next day with a purpose. I brought Tank up to speed on our cases and gave him the authority to use his discretion on anything existing or new. Then I packed up my truck and hit the road.

Yes, flying would have been faster, but I needed the time to gather my thoughts and figure out exactly what I wanted before I got to Nashville.

It was a twenty-two-hour drive, so I stopped for the night before getting back on the road bright and early. Once I was a couple hours outside of Nashville, I called Smith to find out Melody's address.

When he told me she was performing in a honkytonk downtown, I drove straight there, praying I'd make it before she finished her set and left.

By the time I arrived I was ready. I'd searched my feelings, planned it all out, and knew exactly what I was going to say. But when I found myself in the dark room, listening to her sing about how I'd broken her heart, I forgot everything.

She was gorgeous. Amazing. And as she sang, tears streamed down her face.

What was I doing? Was I really fool enough to think she'd want me? Did I deserve another chance?

Then Melody looked up and saw me and I saw a myriad of emotions cross her face before her eyes lit up and she smiled through her tears.

She finished the song and asked, "What are you doing here?"

Everyone around me shifted to look me up and down.

"Is that the guy?" someone shouted.

"Yeah, the one you were just singing about?" A woman asked.

Melody nodded and I felt a shift in the room.

"*Wait!*" I shouted, needing to say my piece before I was found guilty in the court of public opinion.

The room seemed to freeze and as far as I was concerned, everyone evaporated except for me and Melody, who'd stood up and placed her guitar on the stand before walking to front center stage.

I looked up at her and took a deep breath.

"Melody," I began, "I was a fool..."

She gave me a watery smile and nodded in agreement.

"I let my fear over something happening to you overshadow my other feelings for you, and convinced myself you'd be happier, and safer, without me. I thought I'd be able to go back to the way things were before you came into my life, but that's impossible. You brightened up my world and without you, everything's black and white."

Melody hopped off the stage and took a step toward me.

"I'm stealing that for a song," she said with a laugh.

I chuckled. "It's yours. Everything I have and everything I am is yours. I should have told you back in Mason Creek that I wanted you to stay... or take me with you... or some sort of combination of the two. I should have told you that I wanted you to be mine and me to be yours. I should have told you I love you, and I don't want to live my life without you."

She stepped closer and said, "I would have loved hearing that."

"How about now?" I asked, hopeful. "Do you love hearing it now?"

She bit her lower lip and nodded, then bridged the gap between us and gave me a kiss.

The room exploded around us, startling me because I'd honestly forgotten we had an audience.

Melody laughed against my lips.

"I'd like to hear it again," she murmured.

"I love you, Melody Miles," I said, and kissed her with all the love I held in my heart.

When we parted, I held her loosely against me and said, "If there's something *you'd* like to say, *I'd* love to hear it."

"Sorry, I was just basking for a moment," she joked, then lifted her hands to cradle my face and said, "I love you, Lorenzo Fratelli."

THIRTY-SIX

MELODY

"I could get used to this bed."

I looked up at Enzo, loving the feel of his body next to mine, all warm and snuggling after a good night's sleep.

"Yeah?" I asked him, running my fingers lightly over his side and laughing when he jumped.

"Yeah. It's hotel quality," he replied, grasping my hand in his to make me stop.

"I thought your bed was pretty nice too."

"It's okay, nothing like this."

"Hmmm," I murmured, then asked the question that had popped into my head when I wasn't distracted with our make-up sex. "What are you thinking long term?"

"I want to be with you," he said simply, and my heart soared.

"Good, I want to be with you too, but what does that look like?" I prodded.

Enzo took my hand in his and interlaced our fingers.

"I'm open to suggestions," he began. "But I figured

we split our time between here and Mason Creek. I have enough guys who know what they're doing, and Tank is comfortable taking over when I'm not around. I don't have to do as much field work anymore, so I can travel with you if you want. We can build you a studio at the compound, for when we're there, and, I don't know, we'll see what happens and make it work."

"I like that," I admitted, bringing his hand up to my lips. "But I think I'd like to be based out of Mason Creek, build the studio there and live and work in Montana. We'll just keep this place for when we have to be in Nashville but spend most of our time there."

"Really? I thought you loved the city. I don't want you to move for me."

"I know that. But, thinking long term, Mason Creek is where I'd want to raise our family, so..."

He grinned at me. "We're having kids?"

"Eventually, I hope so, yes."

"How many?" he asked.

"I don't know... two? Three? I was an only child, so I don't want to only have one. I know how lonely it can be."

"Two was good for me and Gino. We usually got along pretty well, except when we didn't. I'd be open to three, as well, I just don't want someone to feel left out."

"We don't have to figure it out now," I said with a laugh. "As long as we're on the same page about wanting kids and raising them in Mason Creek. Like I said before, I think it would be a wonderful place to grow up and I want that for them."

"Pops would love it," he said, then looked at me curiously and asked, "But what about your parents? Wouldn't they want to be near their grandkids?"

I lifted one shoulder and said, "They aren't really the little kid type. I'm sure when the kids are old enough to travel, they'll love taking them to shows and going on trips, but they aren't the kind of parents who are going to offer to babysit when we want to go out or take care of them when they're sick."

"Ah."

"Knowing them, though, once we get married and start a family, they'll probably buy a place in Mason Creek for when they come visit. They wouldn't want to stay with us, and I don't think there's a hotel in Mason Creek that would be... up to their standards."

"I see."

Feeling bad about the way I was portraying them, I sat up and amended, "Not that they're like some terrible stuck-up monsters. They're just used to a certain way of life, and they don't really like to sacrifice that."

"You don't have to sell me," Enzo said, pulling me back down so I was laying half on top of him. "I'm sure we'll get along just fine. And I don't mind them having their own place, because I don't really like sharing my space with anyone but you."

"Oh yeah?" I asked, dropping a quick kiss on his lips.

Just then Dixie wiggled between us and licked his face.

"Yeah, and you too, Dixie, of course."

"So, we've talked about where we want to live and agreed to having kids one day. What else?"

"When do you want to go home?" he asked, combing his hands through my hair.

"We've already started on the new album, so I'll have to finish that here, since we don't have a studio there yet. And I have a couple commitments to meet, but maybe by the end of the month? Does that work? If *you* have to go back, it's no problem."

"While you're working, I can start packing up the stuff you'll want moved and take it down then come back for you and Dixie, if that works. And other than that, I can hang out and be your annoying boyfriend."

"Really? I could just hire someone, rather than you do all the work. And you could never be annoying." I traced his lips and added, "You seem way too manly to be called a boyfriend. I think we need to come up with another word."

His lip quirked up and he said, "No need to hire someone to do what I can do myself. Especially when I don't mind doing it. And what did you have in mind? Man friend, lover, conqueror of your heart?"

I started giggling and dropped my head on his chest.

"I was thinking more like, *partner*, you goof," I replied once I caught my breath.

"Partners. I like that," he said, then rolled me over and nuzzled my neck while Dixie ran away.

She knew what we were about to do and wanted no part of it.

EPILOGUE

Melody

"I thought you and Tatum were friends."

Gino looked over at me and shrugged.

"We were, as kids. But since I've been back things have felt kind of... *off*."

We were setting up our spot for fireworks after spending the day at the Fourth of July Festival.

Enzo and Mario had gone to get food and drinks while Gino and I laid out a few blankets to secure a spot in the crowd, which was pretty significant. It seemed like this was one of the events the whole town came out for.

"Why's that?" I asked him, glancing over at Tatum who was sitting with a few friends not far from us.

"Well, my first day back was kind of awkward. I'd got to my dad's the night before and was stopping for coffee on my way to Enzo's, which is where I found the two of you on the couch." He wiggled his eyebrows at me.

I laughed and slapped his arm and prompted, "But before that?"

"I was walking to Java Jitters and there were a couple people walking by. When one of them called my name, I didn't think anything, because just about everyone knows me here, but then I didn't immediately recognize her. I mean, in my defense, she looks totally different than she used to, so if it took me a minute, it should be understandable, right?"

I nodded in agreement, although I could see how Tatum may not see it that way.

"So, I said hi to Darlene, who she was with, and Tate was like, really, Gino, that's how it is? And that's when I knew it was her. I was so shocked I stepped backward and ran into a flowerpot and fell over onto my ass. She didn't laugh, she helped me up, but I was so embarrassed I kind of hurried off and hid inside Java Jitters until they left."

"You *hid*?" I asked. "Well, now I can see why she's been avoiding you. But if you guys were such good friends, you shouldn't let that go because you're embarrassed. You should go talk to her."

"You're right," he said, and when I pointed to where she was sitting, he asked, "What, now?"

"No better time than the present," I replied.

He looked like he wanted to argue but instead ducked his head and shuffled off.

I was still chuckling when Enzo found me and sat down on the blanket. "What's funny?"

"Your brother," I said, gesturing to where he was talking to Tatum. I looked around and asked, "Where's your dad?"

"He got caught up talking to someone from the VFW. He'll be along in a bit," he said, leaning in to kiss me sweetly.

"What'd you get me?" I asked, clapping my hands together as I stared at the provisions.

"As requested, an elephant ear, fried macaroni and cheese balls, French fries with a side of cheese sauce, and a Coke," he said, then met my eyes and said, "You're gonna make yourself sick."

"Nah, I've been training my whole life for this," I joked. "What'd you get for yourself?"

"A cheesesteak, and I figured you'd share your fries."

"Whoa, buddy. There's something you need to learn about me, and fast. I *do not* share fries."

"Are you serious?"

"As a heart attack," I said, crossing my heart with my finger.

He busted out laughing, and as he struggled to breath and clutched his side, he said, "*God, I love you.*"

"That's handy, as I happen to love you, too," I told him, swiping my finger through the powdered sugar on my elephant ear and popping it in my mouth.

"You're the best thing that's ever happened to me," Enzo said, sitting up straighter and then getting on his knees in front of me. "You bring me so much joy and happiness. You make every day count, no matter what we're doing, and you always have a kind word to share. I've never met someone with a heart so pure before, and maybe I came into this a bit jaded, but I swear you make me better each moment we spend together. Even when we aren't together, I want to make you proud."

"Enzo," I said, looking up at him in confusion. "What's happening?"

"Melody, I thought of another word you can call me," he said, reaching into his pocket and pulling out a teal ring box. And when he popped the top open, he said, "*Fiancé*."

"*Oh*," I gasped, my hands flying to my mouth as I gaped at him in shock.

"Melody Marie Miles, please say you'll make me the happiest man on the planet and marry me."

As if he'd planned it, the fireworks started to go off, lighting the sky over our heads in explosions of red, yellow and green.

"Yes, *yes times infinity*, I will marry you!" I cried, getting up to my knees and awkwardly throwing myself at him.

He caught me and held me close, burying his head in my hair.

"I love you."

"I love you, too. Now put the ring on my finger," I cried, laughing through my happy tears.

We shifted back and both looked down as he slid the marquise-cut diamond onto my ring finger.

"It's gorgeous," I told him, a little surprised that he picked out something I would have picked out for myself.

He must have heard it in my tone because he admitted, "I had some help."

"From who?"

"Your mom," Enzo replied, shocking me for the second time that day. "When I went to New York to ask for your father's blessing, your mom and I went ring shopping."

I sat back on my heels, utterly gobsmacked. "When did you go to New York?"

"Remember when I had that trip with Gino to Michigan to show him the ropes on a case?"

I nodded.

"I didn't go to Michigan."

"You brought me back a Red Wings hoodie."

"Gino picked that up for me so you wouldn't get suspicious."

"You were all in on it?" I asked, and he pointed to our right, where Mario, Gino, and Tatum were all standing watching us with big smiles on their face.

Enzo stood and reached down a hand to help me up.

"Very sneaky, Mr. Fratelli," I said, wrapping my arms around his waist. "I love that you went to my parents."

"I hoped it would make you happy, and I wanted them to feel included."

"You are the absolute sweetest man," I said, lifting my head to offer my lips to him. He accepted, kissing me long and thoroughly enough that the people around us started to notice there weren't fireworks in the sky.

I whirled around and grabbed him by the hand then pulled him to the others as I held out my left hand for them to see the ring.

"Look," I exclaimed. *"We're engaged!"*

As soon as I spoke, I realized I'd been too loud, and

before you knew it, the news was making its rounds like a phone tree had been activated.

It didn't take long for everyone in Mason Creek to know the good news, and they were all more than happy to celebrate with us.

THE END

HAVE you already read my first Mason Creek Book Perfect Summer

And, up next from me is Gino's story - Perfect Fall

WANT MORE MASON CREEK?

Keep reading for an excerpt from the next book in the series, Perfect Guy by Fabiola Francisco

Chapter 1 - Madelyn

"Mads-lyn!" I smile when I see Oliver waving at me, standing beside his mom, Camille, and my brother, Levi. Levi, the forever bachelor, has settled down with a single mom, and it has been way too fun watching him fall.

I wave at Oliver before helping the next child on the horse. When I suggested we give horseback rides at the Fourth of July festival in our town, Mason Creek, I didn't think my brothers would go for it. Wilder, the oldest, is who runs our family ranch. The most we do to entertain the public is rent cabins for visitors or anyone needing a home to stay in. However, Roman Wilde Ranch has never participated in a town event, and I thought it'd be fun.

So far, it's been a success. All the children in town

have lined up, buying tickets to ride our horse. Even if it isn't much, it's some money to add to the ranch's finances.

Working at the ranch is definitely not my dream job, but I'm helping my brothers and taking part in our family legacy. That's priceless. Right now, it's what I need.

When I made the decision to move back to Mason Creek after finishing my Masters in Architecture, I knew it would be to do something else than I had planned my entire life. Circumstances in life make us take detours, and I'm working on being okay with that, even after being back home for six months.

I don't have time for thoughts of the past to plague my mind. I finish the ride, smiling at the young boy and thanking the parents before giving Juliet an apple. Levi's horse is gentle, and she's used to working with Oliver, so we knew she'd be perfect for today's event.

"Are you doing okay? Do you want a break?" Wilder walks into the small pen we set up to give the rides.

"I'm good. I told you guys I'd be responsible for this, and I'm keeping my word." I nod and stand my ground.

Wilder chuckles, shaking his head. He lifts his hat, brushing his hair back before readjusting his Stetson.

"If you want a water break or something, let me know. I'm around."

"Thanks. I only have a few more hours left." I look around the festival. Booths, banners, and balloons are all around Town Square. The main roads are cut off for foot traffic, and we have a ton of tourists.

Wilder doesn't like city folks, so it's probably better if I stick to this, seeing as a lot of the kids are from the city.

"I'll bring you something from The Sweet Spot and a coffee from Java Jitters."

"Thanks. Can you make the coffee a frappe?" The Sweet Spot is our local bakery, and Joy, the owner, is a good friend of mine. I live for anything she bakes, and coffee is a main food group in my diet. Between early hours when I lived at home and long study nights at university, coffee has always been my saving grace.

"Coming right up." He taps the bill of my cap, and I swat his arm. I fix my hat and call over the next child, getting lost in the job I have to do.

I was raised around animals, so this is my happy place. Riding horses, rounding cattle, helping birth lambs, or anything else related to animals, you name it. My parents thought I'd grow up to be a vet, which would've made more sense, but I have a dream of creating homes people will build memories in or businesses so people can accomplish their own dreams.

After closing up the rides, I head to find my family. I have about an hour to enjoy the festival before the fireworks. Hearing the music, I walk toward the stage where Tucker Simms, our local musician, is singing an older country song.

"Mads-lyn!" Oliver races to me.

"Oof." My arms come to his back when he crashes into me. "How's Juliet?" He looks up at me.

"She's good and resting now. I thought you were going to ride when I saw you near the pen."

"Mommy said to let the other kids ride since I gets to spend my days with Juliet." He shrugs.

"That's real kind of you." I ruffle his head. "Where is

your mommy?" I scan the area and find my parents waving at me.

"She's dancing with Horseman."

I chuckle at his nickname for Levi. He must've been with my parents. My mom watches Oliver since there wasn't a spot in pre-school when he and Camille moved into town. She's going to miss him when he starts kindergarten this fall.

"Hey," Joy meets up with me.

"Hi, did you just close up?"

"I did. I'm ready to sleep for twelve hours. Thank goodness I decided to close the bakery tomorrow."

"Maybe it's time you hire some help?" I lift my brows. Joy's stubborn and likes doing everything herself the way her grandmother did, but even she had help. Her grandmother helps her for now, popping in during the day to relieve some of the workload, but it's not enough. Joy runs the place all alone.

"Brayden says the same thing," she says of her boyfriend. "He says Grandma is getting too old to come and help me. Not that I'd tell my grandma that. She'd smack him across the head."

I laugh, knowing that to be true. Holding Oliver's hand, we walk toward my parents.

"How are you?" My mom asks.

"Good. Tired." I suppress a yawn.

"Well, everyone's talking about the horse ride. They loved it," my dad comments with a proud smile.

"I think so," I nod.

"How about you, Joy?" My mom asks her.

"It was great. We sold out, which is awesome."

"That's great," my mom and I say at the same time.

"Mads-lyn, will you dance wif me?" Oliver looks up at me with round eyes that make me melt. I love that he combines my nickname with my full name.

"Of course, buddy." I spin him around before lifting him.

Oliver laughs and holds on to my shoulders, looking around with a wide smile. He's the most adorable little boy I've met. After everything he's been through, he still has a kind heart.

"Mommy, look! I dance like you," he calls out to Camille, who laughs and nods.

"You are, baby." She looks at me and mouths, *Thank you.*

We spin around to the beat of the faster country song. My dance partner is the best ever. The four-year-old won't disappoint me the way adults do. His pout is exaggerated when the song ends.

"I want 'nother!" He holds on tight to my shoulders.

"We'll wait for the next song." My arms ache from holding him and moving around, but I'll never let him know that. I've spent the last few months getting to know Oliver and babysitting him whenever Levi and Camille go out. He's become my buddy, and I'll do anything for him.

"Yay!" He shrieks when the next song begins.

We dance another song before he's tired of dancing and runs to his mom. I stand alone in the middle of dancing couples.

A deep chuckle makes me jolt. "That kid is too cute."

I turn and look at Canaan, Joy's brother.

"He is," I nod.

"By the way, great job on those plans you brought in the other day. My boss loved the suggestions you made."

"Really?" My eyes widen.

Canaan is a carpenter for a construction company in a nearby town. When he approached me about a month ago, asking if I'd be interested in working on a project since their regular architect wasn't available, I agreed to meet his boss. I'm still jaded from what happened at the university, but this was a good opportunity. It'd allow me a chance to work on something that wasn't permanent and see if my heart was still in it after everything.

"Yeah," he nods. "Moving the kitchen to the other side allowed to make the rooms bigger, and the clients loved the breakfast nook with the bay windows."

Pride swells in my chest. Maybe I can have both—working at the ranch and still doing what I love.

"I'm so happy to hear that!" I swing my arms around Canaan. "Thanks."

"Uh...you're welcome." He pats my back awkwardly.

"Sorry," I step back as heat fills my cheeks. "I got excited. Anyway, I'm gonna go...see where my brothers are." I hook a thumb over my shoulder in search of an escape plan.

"It's okay, just caught me off-guard." Canaan laughs, running a hand through his hair.

Canaan is older than me, and being Joy's brother, I never really allowed myself to notice him. By the time I was in high school and interested in checking guys out, Canaan was working and dating women his age with all the right curves. Not to mention, I was always a tomboy growing up. That hasn't changed much, but I did expand my wardrobe and girly knowledge in college.

Deep down, though, I'll always choose worn jeans and cowboy boots and spend my time outdoors rather than perfecting my makeup skills.

But now that I've spent more time with him and I'm not a little girl, I've definitely admired his strong body, muscular arms, and the way he fills out his worn jeans. Seeing him work with his hands and different tools is a sight for sore eyes. I have to remind myself that he's a friend, someone I've known almost my entire life, and ignore any fluttering happening in my belly.

ACKNOWLEDGMENTS

To my fellow Mason Creek authors, thanks so much for including me in this project and being such wonderful collaborators.

To Lydia and Megan with HEA PR and More, thanks for putting up with me and helping us spread the word about Mason Creek. It's been wonderful working with you!

To Sarah Paige, the genius behind our beautiful covers. Thanks for helping bring Mason Creek to life.

To Katie, my *girl in the chair*, thanks for your support and encouragement.

To Ann and Raine, thanks for reading and giving me your feedback.

ABOUT THE AUTHOR

Bethany Lopez is a USA Today Bestselling author of more than seventy published works, as both Bethany Lopez and DJ Bryce, and has been publishing since 2011. She's a lover of all things romance, which she incorporates into the books she writes, no matter the genre.

When she isn't reading or writing, she loves spending time with family and traveling whenever possible.

Bethany can usually be found with a cup of coffee or glass of wine at hand, and will never turn down a cupcake!

To learn more about upcoming events and releases, sign up for my newsletter.

www.bethanylopezauthor.com
bethanylopezauthor@gmail.com

Follow her at https://www.bookbub.com/authors/bethany-lopez *to get an alert whenever she has a new release, preorder, or discount!*

ALSO BY BETHANY LOPEZ

Contemporary Romance:

Laugh, Swoon, and Fall in Love: Romance Series Starters Box Set

The Jilted Wives Club Trilogy

Starter Wife

Trophy Wife

Work Wife

Backup Wife

Accidental Wife - Preorder

Mason Creek Series

Perfect Summer

Perfect Christmas Anthology

Perfect Hideaway

Perfect Fall - Coming Soon

A Time for Love Series

Prequel - 1 Night - FREE

8 Weeks - FREE

21 Days

42 Hours

15 Minutes

10 Years

3 Seconds

7 Months

For Eternity - Novella

Night & Day - Novella

Time for Love Series Box Set

Time to Risk

The Lewis Cousins Series

Too Tempting

Too Complicated

Too Distracting

Too Enchanting

Too Dangerous

The Lewis Cousins Box Set

Too Enticing - Short

Three Sisters Catering Trilogy

A Pinch of Salt

A Touch of Cinnamon

A Splash of Vanilla

Three Sisters Catering Trilogy Box Set

Frat House Confessions

Frat House Confessions: Ridge

Frat House Confessions: Wes

Frat House Confessions: Brody

Frat House Confessions 1 - 3 Box Set

Frat House Confessions: Crush - Coming Soon

Romantic Comedy/Suspense:

Delilah Horton Series

Always Room for Cupcakes - FREE

Cupcake Overload

Lei'd with Cupcakes

Cupcake Explosion

Cupcakes & Macaroons - Honeymoon Short - FREE

Lei'd in Paradise - Novella (Carmen & Bran)

Crazy for Cupcakes - Coming Soon

Women's Fiction:

More than Exist

Unwoven Ties

Short Stories/Novellas:

Contemporary:

Christmas Come Early

Harem Night

Reunion Fling

An Inconvenient Dare

Snowflakes & Country Songs

Fool for You - FREE

Desert Alpha (Lady Boss Press Navy SEAL Novella)

Fantasy:

Leap of Faith

Beau and the Beastess

Cookbook:

Love & Recipes

Love & Cupcakes

Children's:

Katie and the North Star

Young Adult:

Stories about Melissa – series

Ta Ta for Now!

xoxoxo

Ciao

TTYL

Stories About Melissa Books 1 - 4

With Love

Adios

Young Adult Fantasy:

Nissa: a contemporary fairy tale

New Adult:

Friends & Lovers Trilogy

Make it Last

I Choose You

Trust in Me

Indelible

Made in the USA
Middletown, DE
19 May 2023